TAKE THE SUN WITH YOU
AND OTHER STORIES

TAKE

the

SUN

with

YOU

AND OTHER STORIES

GREGORY ALLEN MENDELL

Take The Sun With You
And Other Stories

Also By The Author

Finding the Elsewhere

The Sting of Immortality, published in *Spring Into SciFi: 2021 Edition*, Cloaked Press, LLC

For all the teachers, writers, friends, and family who have taught me so much.

About The Book

Here are ten tales where the fantastical digs its fangs into the possible. The science behind these stories is weird but real, though no limits bind the imagination. At the heart of this collection are core fears about the future, with characters thrown into strangeness while exploring love and hope for better days.

Contents

A TRAGIC LOSS OF DECOHERENCE

– When Billy Teal meets quantum fruit flies, he must decide whether to fit in or follow the many worlds of his heart's desire.

Billy Teal died three times last week. But he kept chasing her.

Through the wave of mindless commuters jostling past him, he saw her one block down across Michigan Avenue. He pushed through the crowd.

"Annag."

She didn't respond. He forced his way into a gap and ran while grasping the orange fiber-optic cables around his neck. He wanted to pull them, to dislodge his earbuds and let his braincase drop into his shirt. But then she'd die and he'd be left with the bloody mess, sent off for another brainwashing. He tried to concentrate. He didn't want this universe to split, whatever happened.

He approached the intersection. Two seconds were left on the walk sign and she was moving away. His mouth opened to yell—but he was drowned out by a blaring horn. Red warning signals beat against his retinas, stopping him cold, as the street parted down the middle. The pavement rolled back with the thunderous sound of concrete scraping against steel to create a wide opening. Damn sky-train. He clenched the orange cables again and thought-on his City Traffic Flow App. He literally couldn't move. Neither could anyone else at the crossing.

Ghost eyes flickered from a little girl squeezing to get between the legs of a middle-aged couple. Impossible, Billy thought, unless her parents were stupid and her CTFA was off.

Tracks rose up through the opening. In a moment the sky-train would pass like a bullet into the blue, raking little Ghost Eyes to the side. She was too close.

Billy's legs twitched. Screw it, he thought. CTFA off, authorization twelve thirty-four. Thank goodness most cities never changed the default password.

He ripped the orange cables away from his body, pulling the electrodes from his ears. He'd have to risk staying in this universe, risk losing Annag, for now.

Rushing into the street, he scooped the girl into his arms and angled around the hole with the emerging tracks, reaching the other side. His heart beat fast, but he didn't feel heroic. After putting the girl down, he jumped up, trying to see farther down the block.

Then he knelt by the girl and the Emulate under his shirt flopped into the gutter. With it came the orange cables, and blood dripped from the electrodes at the ends no longer attached to his ears.

Behind him the train blasted past. Gone.

Everyone started moving again, including the girl's parents. They crossed, took her by the elbow, and whisked her away. Gone.

A grade-school boy wearing an academy uniform bumped into him. "Oooh. You're a bio-brain?" The boy made a gagging sound and ran away. Gone.

"Freak," a faceless passerby said. Gone.

"Get a wash," another said. Gone.

And Annag? Gone.

* * *

"Billy, please give me your braincase."

He blinked at the dark-haired brainwasher in the open lab coat sitting across from him. "Here." He handed her his Emulate still attached to the orange cables with the electrodes.

She used a cloth to clean away the dirt and blood. Then she put a glass cylinder on her desk, filled it with a clear blue liquid, and plopped in the Emulate.

"Are you having troubling self-locating?" she asked.

"Maybe."

"Billy, I'm not just a brainwasher. I'm a therapist too."

"Sure." He shrugged.

"Most people adapt. But one in a million has a problem. You're not alone."

"No ... no, I'm not," Billy said. "There are thousands of me's out there ... millions actually ... I know." He pulled an apple from his pocket and put it on the desk. "Care for a bite?"

"Hmm, haven't seen one of those in a while. They're not allowed in here."

"Huh?"

"Besides, I don't eat any kind of fruit, not even at home. I've come to dislike it."

"Really? In most other universes you ... never mind. Wanna know something?"

"What Billy?"

"As soon as you give me my brain back, I'll split again. It's like this. I've given you apples, pears, bananas, a raisin—whatever the stand at the market has—and your hair's been brown, yellow, red, green, blue, you name it. Hah—that's funny ... because your name—it's either Angel, or Jade, or Keysha, or—"

"I'm Dr. Nina Estrella." She tugged her ponytail over her shoulder.

He twirled the apple by its stem. "Your looks change too." His gaze moved across her top and he tried not to linger. Just checking I still have a pulse, he imagined explaining to Annag.

"Billy." Nina's tone was firm and told him to cut the crap. She pushed her ponytail back and tapped the temple of her glasses. "Billy ... I can help."

"Okay. But I meet Annag in every universe. Her name—it's always the same."

"I know."

"You know?" Despair rushed through his veins. He picked up the apple and threw it against the wall. "I've been here a million times. But how can *you* know that?"

* * *

"So, Billy, tell me again. How does it happen?"

Billy was relieved to see it was still Nina. Of course, it had to be her. She'd scanned him and sent him away to let his bio-brain rest while his computer-brain had a good soak.

It was so stupid, he thought. How could anyone think the gray and white matter between his ears wasn't real? It was, damn it. Everyone had bio-brains before—so why did everyone act like having your mind uploaded to an Emulate was as natural as cottage pie?

Why?

Why did keeping your bio-brain make you a freak?

Sure, most people adapted and forgot about the fatty bio one after it was removed through the nose. But did that make them better persons? Weren't the empty-heads the real freaks?

If only he could make them realize his bio-brain was superior. For one thing, it had no problem self-locating. Once it was in a universe, it stayed there. And if the universe split, he went in one direction, not all directions at once. He should be able to explain that to Nina. Right?

Not that it mattered. When she plugged him back into his computer mind—for more adaptation practice—he'd make the universe split. Then he could look for Annag again.

Nina drummed her fingers and Billy finally responded.

4

"You want me to tell you how it happens? Again?"

"Yes." Nina looked genuinely curious.

"It's easy," Billy said. "Last time, I also had an apple. Now imagine the odds of eating an apple, or anything, and choking to death."

"I'm sure *that* can happen—"

"To the same person? Millions of times? And don't even get me started on weird traffic accidents ..." Billy tried to get his voice under control. It wasn't her fault she didn't understand. "Impossible? Not when anything that can happen, does ... in some universe."

"That's not how it works," Nina said. "One has to consider the allowed quantum states."

"But if all it takes is an apple ..." Billy leaned back in his chair and put his feet on her desk. "If all it takes is an apple to cause me to enter a death spiral through the multiverse—"

"It's not really the multiverse," Nina continued in lecture mode. "And the universe is inferred to split only when the possible states of one quantum observable become entangled with the almost countless quantum states of the environment. Simply choking on an apple won't cause a split. Regardless, even if you perceive a split, there's only one universe."

"There's not—"

"Billy, it's what I was telling you yesterday. There's only one wave function with many branches forming what we call many worlds. Luckily most of us are never aware of the branching but quickly self-locate to a probable world, experiencing life as taking place in one world with a consistent history. You will too, once you adapt." Nina looked down. "Except—"

"Except, to me it's not one universe. It's not one history. It becomes all of them at once." Billy put his feet down. He interlaced his fingers across his forehead and pulled them back over his ears. He felt beads of sweat on his brow. His calm exterior slipped away.

Nina smoothed an eyebrow and looked up. "As I was saying ... except, because your brain is not dissipating properly, your state remains coherent."

"If you ask me, it's just the opposite of coherent. But there is ... there is one constant."

"Annag?"

"Sometimes we meet, stay together for a day or two. She's like me ... lost, trying to adapt. We can help each other. I'm sure of it. But ..."

"Yes?"

"But one of us always dies. If I pull out my earbuds, or she does, to permanently self-locate—we can't seem to both do it at the same time—the other dies soon after. So, I have no choice. I have to get brainwashed and plugged in. Then I wait for a split—or cause it—and go searching for her again."

"Because?"

Billy laid his arms on the table. "Because? Because I have to find her." He put his head on the desk and stretched his neck as if he were waiting for an executioner. "Go ahead, plug me in." He sighed and watched Nina stand up from his sideways view.

"You're right, Billy. Finding Annag might help. But first, you can help us."

"What?"

"Follow me."

* * *

The fruit fly room was in the basement. In all the universes Billy had fathomed, he'd never seen a room like it.

"This is why fruit isn't allowed in the building," Nina explained. "But before we start, I have to ask you one thing. Are you in love with Annag?"

"Maybe? I hardly know her. But when we meet, I feel like ... you'll laugh ..."

"Trust me, I won't."

Billy shrugged. "Okay, I feel like I've met the person I'm meant for ... my soulmate."

Nina laughed.

"I'm disappointed in you, Doc," Billy said. Still, he started to like Nina. "So, what's all this?" He pointed to a box surrounded by two coils of wire and connected to a hose.

"It's the experiment, Billy. The one I said you could help us with. It can help you too."

"Yeah?" He surveyed a control panel closer to him. On it, a button was marked 'start' and next to it was an old-fashioned watch with only a second hand. There was also a large wooden lever just waiting to be pulled. He caught something out of the corner of his eye and found the other end of the hose. "Why is the gas cylinder over there marked poison? You're going the help me split the universe without me choking to death this time?"

"Not exactly. You're too big to fit in the box, anyway."

Billy clenched his hand and coughed into it. "You're starting to scare me."

Nina smiled. "I'm joking."

"I thought so. But really, tell me about it. You don't have to dumb it down. I've been around ... you know ..."

"Well, this is the fruit-fly room. There are some in that box. There's also a cold trap in there with a single hydrogen atom. The coils put that atom in a rotating magnetic field, setting up resonance with the atom's proton nucleus. It's like an MRI scanner. See that glass tube linked to the electronics sticking out of the back of the box?"

Billy leaned a little closer. "Some sort of sensor?"

"Right. The proton has a spin with a corresponding magnetic moment that interacts with the rotating field of the coils. This can cause the proton's spin to flip, and when it does, it emits a particle of light, a photon. And if the sensor picks that up, it causes the poison gas to release."

Billy shook his head. "Nina, you lost me. I mean, I sorta get MRI. At least I've heard of it. But why in heaven's name are you doing this?" He laughed. "Did the fruit flies axe murder a watermelon or something? And don't say it—"

"It's for science, Billy."

"Okay, you said it—but I'll bet animal-rights groups aren't happy about this."

"Let me finish. You see, when you push the button on the control panel it starts the magnetic resonance and the timer. At time zero, there's a fifty-fifty chance the proton's spin will flip. The fruit flies then have a fifty-fifty chance of being dead or alive."

"Wait, I get it. It's like that famous quantum cat. But this time it's to do with fruit flies?"

"Very good, Billy. However, in the example you're thinking of, the cat gets entangled with a radioactive atom with a fifty-fifty chance of decaying and releasing poison, so the cat goes into a superposition of being alive and dead at the same time."

"Until someone opens the box." Billy grinned. "Is that what the lever does?"

"Yes, but let me explain. By using magnetic resonance, we control the probability of the spin flipping. It doesn't stay fifty-fifty. Instead, the probability oscillates between zero and one. And we've arranged it so when the timer reaches fifteen seconds, the probably is one. That is, at the fifteen-second mark it's certain the fruit flies will die."

"Okay, you're losing me again. The fruit flies always die?"

"Only if you open the box at fifteen seconds. If you don't open the box, the probability keeps changing and goes back to fifty-fifty when the timer gets to thirty seconds. And it keeps decreasing until at exactly forty-five seconds the probability is zero that the spin has flipped. Of course, to make it work the sensor has to have almost no electrical resistance and only a few molecules of the poison are allowed to go in. This keeps things reversible. Get it?"

"Maybe." Billy knew quantum ideas were weird. But this sounded completely wacko.

"If you pull the lever at the forty-five-second mark the fruit flies are guaranteed to be alive. But if you pull the lever at the fifteen-second mark the fruit flies are guaranteed to be dead. Thus, waiting thirty seconds brings them back to life."

"You resurrect them?"

"Yes, so to speak. Or, we could—except for decoherence."

"Oh—that's the word." Billy turned away. Anxiety rippled down his spine as it twisted. "That's what every therapist says. I've lost decoherence."

"Exactly. In a normal brain, in any dissipative system really, the coherent superposition effectively collapses when the system interacts irreversibly with its environment."

"And I should self-locate to a world with a consistent history. I've heard it all before. I'd be fine, *except* my computer-brain—"

"Stays coherent, experiences all the possibilities, all the branches, until you land in one at random." Nina reached out and took Billy's hand. "And all consistency is lost, which I know must be very difficult for you. So, let me help."

"How?"

"Your computer-brain, Billy—in some ways it's too perfect. Too pure. It's not dissipative enough. And since the government considers your soul to be in your Emulate, the real you *is* in there. We can't destroy it. We can't start over and give you a new one. But we can fix it."

"I see." Billy wondered why in every world there was always some reason it wasn't possible to destroy his computer-brain and start over. "But killing fruit flies? That's okay?"

"For science, like I said. Though let me finish my explanation. When we try the experiment with old-fashioned fruit flies, no matter when we pull the lever, if it's after fifteen seconds they're always dead. At the fifteen-second mark, their bio-brains always decohere into the dead state. Decoherence gives us the experience of the classical, non-quantum world. But ..."

"I knew there'd be one."

"But, when we replace a fly's bio-brain with a special computer one, one made to stay coherent, we can resurrect it every time by pulling the lever at exactly the forty-five-second mark. You see, fruit flies were one of the first non-trivial organisms to have every neuron in their brains mapped. So, we've figured out how to reproduce your problem."

"In a fruit fly?"

"Yes."

Billy tried to gather his thoughts. Maybe there *was* something in Nina's scientific babble that could help him. "With a fruit fly, a special one, don't you see it half alive and half dead?"

"No. No, we don't. Our minds, I mean those of us with normal computer minds, undergo decoherence. We observe it to be alive or dead, in accordance with the probabilities at the time we pull the lever. But theoretically our special computer-brain flies experience different branches of our universe simultaneously. Just like you."

"Okay, so when I'm plugged in again, are you saying if I pull the lever my world will split with the flies? Is that what you want me to do? You want me to tell you what that's like? Because I can already tell you about that, so—"

"It's better than that, Billy. We want to resurrect you!"

* * *

Billy wasn't sure he believed any of it. He hopped in an eggshell and let it take him to the suburbs, back to the address where he'd stayed last night. His therapists always found one of his relatives nearby and arranged for him to get a bed and some food. Nina had done the same.

This time the relative looked like his mom. At least like the one he knew before he got his Emulate and started to split. His dad had died before this. So, it made sense she was alone.

Last night she didn't seem to know him, though she'd given him dinner and pointed him to a bed. She'd been on autopilot, doing chores, while her mind lived whatever dream was playing in her head—or really, in the Emulate hanging around her neck. Billy didn't like to think about it. He never got used to the idea that other people's heads were empty.

At least she hadn't asked him where his earbuds were.

This time, after crossing the brown-patched lawn, he entered the old two-storied house and found her in the kitchen.

"Mom, you listening?"

He looked at her round body wrapped in a farmhouse dress and apron, her sagging arms rolling dough. "My baby," she muttered. She turned to Billy. Her smooth face was punctured with vacant eyes and framed by curls. She pointed the rolling pin up the stairs.

"Yes, I know, my bed's up there," Billy said. "But I'm hungry."

His mom, or whoever she was, started to rummage through a drawer of cookie cutters.

"Mom? It's me." Billy stared at the woman's back. "Mom?"

He left the kitchen and made for the worn steps that led up. He'd told Nina he needed a night to sleep on the offer she'd made him. He might as well start on that now.

Hauling himself up the stairs, his body ached. There was too much to think about. When he reached the landing, he knew he was tired. Tired of it all.

"Hey Billy."

The voice came from the bathroom, its door half-open. He rushed in.

"Don't look."

"Annag?" He stared at her in the bath, all covered in bubbles. "You're here?"

She looked up and smiled. "Walter sent me."

"Who?"

"My therapist, Dr. Walter Yang. He said I might find you here. So, I waited downstairs but then I decided to clean up ... you know, because ..."

Billy didn't know. This had never happened before. "Why?"

"I was talking with Walter about how we've never been intimate ... never been together long enough—"

"Your rules, not mine."

"He thought I'd learn why if I came here." Annag seemed happy. "So, here I am. Though I was planning to get dressed. And I imagined we'd talk a bit first ... you know ..."

"Okay." Billy backed out of the bathroom. Scared. Delighted. Her earbuds were in, but with a little fooling around, who knew? Maybe they'd come out if he was gentle and all. Maybe they could both permanently locate in this universe—two bio-brains in love—together, forever. He brushed back his hair. He wanted to tidy up too. But he didn't want her to think he'd gone away, so he tried to make conversation. "You've never mentioned a therapist before ..."

There was no response. Instead, he heard a whirring. It seemed to come from below the tub—probably from his mom running a mixer in the kitchen.

Then like thunder from above, the roof crashed in.

Wood splintered in all directions. A sky-train flashed past him with a roar from hell, tearing the bathroom away and leaving a path of destruction. He remained on the landing and looked down into a smoking crater filled with twisted metal and debris.

Half the house. Gone.

His mother. Gone.

Annag. Gone.

All hope. Gone.

* * *

Nina sat lecturing him.

"You're twenty-nine. You can't expect to keep your bio-brain forever. Your memories, they're starting to go. Dementia, that's what awaits you if you don't adapt. So, you see, you really should give it a try."

"I do see." Billy looked around the big box he was in with Nina. "It's the same set up, only I'm in the experiment and get to pull the lever myself." His tone was flat. "And plugged into my coherent computer mind, if I wait forty-five seconds I'm guaranteed to live. I get it."

"Yes, but after fifteen seconds, you'll know what it's like to die."

"No biggie for me, as I've explained. But this time ... if I time it right ..." Billy looked into Nina's eyes. There was still some light behind them.

Then he thought of Annag. If it didn't work, he'd die like usual and split right out of this world, this universe, as it seemed to him. That would be okay. This universe could die too, for all he cared. But maybe ... maybe he could finish things ... once and for all. "If I time it right ..." he repeated.

"Yes, Billy," Nina said, "you can live. However, you'll be dead at the fifteen-second mark in every world and it won't be confusing, at least for a split-second. Forgive the pun. Then you'll go back into a confused superposition of being alive and dead until the forty-five-second mark. That's when you must pull the lever."

"And I'll be resurrected? And you want me to tell you what it's really like to be dead?" Billy wasn't sure about that part. Nina had shown him some equations, but of course that didn't help. "So, you win the Nobel Prize or whatever. But what does that do for me?"

"We think ..." Nina bit one of her nails. "I shouldn't tell you this. But I have to. Billy, we think the cause of your problem is related to Annag."

"Yes, Annag ..." He shook his head. "She has the same problem."

"Listen. That math I showed you. It indicates your quantum state is almost anticorrelated with hers. That's why you can never be together for more than a few days. The small probability of it grows weaker until there's a split where you die and she lives, or vice versa. Let me explain. Though I shouldn't—"

"Please, you can't stop now."

"Then listen. If you pull the lever at the fifteen-second mark you'll die for sure, not just in this world but in all of them. And stay dead. Forever. But—"

"But if I wait for forty-five seconds, I'll live in all of them? Forever?"

"Exactly, or at least until your natural death. More importantly, your computer mind will stop having problems self-locating. You'll be cured."

Billy wrapped his mind around this. "And it'll be worth it? I'll live and be—"

"Normal, yes—like us."

A rage surged inside Billy. Then he knew what he had to do. He breathed hard and placed a firm grip on the lever. "Okay. You've convinced me. Let's do this damned thing."

* * *

After Nina plugged his earbuds in, she left the room and the door closed.

Billy stared for moment at the control panel then pushed the start button.

Pull the lever at exactly the forty-five-second mark, she'd said. Then he'd live.

He watched the timer's second hand, heard it tick, three, four, five, ...

But she'd said something else. He was anti-correlated with Annag. Her state, the opposite of his. There was another way.

Through the blur of worlds, he counted the ticks ... eight, nine, ten, ...

At the fifteen-second mark he'd pull the lever.

Then he'd die.

For sure.

In every world.

Forever.

"And Annag, you'll live!" he shouted. "Forever!"

With the fifteenth tick he pulled the lever with every muscle fiber he could muster.

* * *

"It's unbelievable, Nina."

She looked at her colleague, Dr. Yang, and at Billy's slumped body. "It's my fault. I should have guessed he might try to sacrifice his own life to save Annag's."

"You said you told him too much." Dr. Yang touched Billy's shoulder.

"Not everything. I couldn't bring myself to tell him who Annag really was."

"That she was him? I discovered that too. She'd told me about looking for a Billy Teal and your scan of him came up in our records. After scanning her, I knew."

Nina turned. "Walter, would you want to know? That at conception the universe split?

"That in one he was Billy? In the other, Annag? I was her therapist—I thought she should know. That's why I sent her to the mother's house, so she could go there to

15

discover it herself. Otherwise, they were headed for trouble ..."

"If only I had known Annag was seeing you, it could have been different." Nina paused. "But what happened to her? You said she was the victim of an accident?"

"Yes, with a sky-train. Heard about it just before I came in here."

Nina shook her head. "And it happened where I sent Billy?" She began to pace. "Their split, it wasn't complete. They're entangled, almost completely anticorrelated. It's so awful."

"Awful, yes. But look at him now. Dead, even though the gas didn't go off."

"Hmm, the lever must have jammed." Nina stopped and motioned with her arm. "But he pulled so hard. Who would have thought it could break like that?"

"And impale him?" Dr. Yang pulled Billy back, revealing where the half of the lever still attached to the floor had stuck in his chest. "His dumb luck."

Then Nina laughed. "No. No, it wasn't luck. Not for him. He could choke to death on a raisin. He'd told me so ... the universe has given him another chance to find Annag."

"No gas, but he still died." Dr. Yang's earbuds lit up. "But there's a chance he'd live?"

"Exactly," Nina said. "He would have split. I can feel it. He's still out there, out there in a million worlds, still looking for her." She closed her eyes. "God speed, Billy. God speed."

* * *

Through the wave of mindless commuters jostling past him he saw her. He couldn't remember how he'd gotten here. But there she was ...

TAKE THE SUN WITH YOU

– When diplomatic teams travel to the center of the Milky Way, a clone and an AI must find where they belong in the far future.

"Cherry," Daeisy called out a split second before the ice cream ball hit Carbon's face.

Carbon ducked behind the hundred-meter-long, chrome-lined, mahogany counter in the Great Hall's ice cream parlor and licked a sticky bit from the corner of his mouth. The zing of the cherry flavor helped revive him, as did the sting of the impact. Luckily, the ice cream was soft, like frozen yogurt, and he was a tough clone. But why had Daeisy chosen this way to wake him? Was this iteration of the Dedicated Artificial Emotional Intelligent System even more exuberant than the last one?

Carbon began to remember. He and Daeisy always came to the Great Hall for ice cream, though usually at the end of the emissary convention. And after spending two weeks with the other one hundred ninety-three diplomats, the tension of the serious discussions always melted away into silly fits of laughter, followed by someone starting an ice cream ball fight.

How long had it been since the last time? Carbon wasn't sure. He recalled one thing, the fact that his Daeisy, the one partnered with him, the one he simply called Daeisy, had the best aim.

He peeked and saw she was on the east side of the hall searching for another flavor. He moved down his

17

side of the hall, peering at the kaleidoscope of colors in round cartons on ice and the labels on the sneeze guards. He found Chocolate Mousse, scooped a sphere into his throwing hand, and sprang up. "Take this." He threw at the center of Daeisy's crisp blue apron.

She dodged but stuck out a free hand, caught Carbon's projectile, and gave it a taste. "Yum," she said before firing back with her other hand. "Curry."

Another direct hit. The spicy flavor mixed in with the cream was unique. Carbon imagined his face probably looked like the time he'd attended the Indian Festival of Colors where everyone was smeared with turmeric and other powders in a celebration of love. Daeisy would really enjoy a festival like that.

For his next move, Carbon crouched down and looked up. He studied the holo-screen's scrolling list of languages: Arabic, Bengali, Catalan, Chinese, English, Fijian, French, German, Greek, Gujarati, Hebrew, Hindi, Hungarian, Indonesian, Japanese, Korean, Malayalam, Marathi, Oriya, Portuguese, Polynesian, Quechua, Romanian, Russian, Siksika, Spanish, Swahili, Swedish, Thai, and Zulu, alongside a much longer list of countries, and next to a seemingly endless list of flavors to choose from.

Then another soft orb hit Carbon on the top of his head, obviously lobbed along a perfect parabolic path to its target. It made him realized the 'fun' he was having with Daeisy could go on for a while, and he was getting too old for this. "Truce," he called out. "I'm awake now."

"We've barely started on the first million flavors," Daeisy said with a friendly taunt in her voice. "But follow me." She took off the apron, draped it over one of the hundreds of spinning stools with matching blue cushions, and walked toward the entrance to the hall.

Carbon trailed behind her and entered a quadrangle where wide sidewalks, lined by silhouettes of trimmed shrubs and trees, disappeared into the dark. It was a warm summer night, late, with no lights ahead except for the mobile screen in Daeisy's hand. She touched something and things got darker. Glancing back, Carbon saw the lights in the hall were out.

"Gaze up," Daeisy said.

Carbon did and almost fell over. Crisp and clear, a moonless, impossible sky was filled with millions of stars brighter than any Carbon had ever seen. "How long?" Carbon asked.

"Longer than you think," Daeisy replied. "We had a recent setback and had to put the humans into a Hilbert box again. They're in their latest pandemic and facing another round of climate change in the simulation. Even after the switch from fossil fuels to geothermal and other renewables, humans always find a way. Try saying deforestation, hydrochlorofluorocarbons, and sulfur hexafluoride three times fast. But with a few tweaks we can get them past this."

"We always have. Millions of pandemics, millions of world wars, a thousand climate crises, a hundred supervolcanoes—after sixty million years, we've seen it all. What's another ten million on top of that? But the sky ..." Carbon blinked to correct his vision. "The sky ..."

"It's been a lot longer than ten million years this time. That's why it took longer to revive you. I'm sure you've guessed that by now."

Carbon's head throbbed. His senses swirled as if his head had been run though a ringer, the last drop of his consciousness squeezed from his folded brain, before his memories were poured back into him and reconnected, returning him to awareness. But the sky ... it said it all.

Daeisy's eyes examined him in the light of her screen, her long lashes waving slowly, showing concern.

"So, we're here," he finally said.

"Yes," Daeisy said. "Were here, ninety million years since the last convention, one hundred fifty million years since our journey's start. Everyone else is up. But you were harder to wake this time and I used the ice cream. So much fun." She grinned. "There's one more thing. Can you find it?"

Carbon knew what Daeisy meant. He scanned the sky. "Yes." He pointed at a ring of light about the size of the Moon.

"That's it," Daeisy said, "the Einstein Ring."

"Just like the simulations." Carbon's thoughts crushed down on him like the weight of the four million solar mass black hole at the Milky Way's center. Yes, they had arrived.

And soon he'd never see Daeisy again.

* * *

Daeisy opened the copy of her diamond diary.

Carbon had never seen it. He was resting in the next room. Maybe she'd show it to him before they parted. Maybe not. As a Dedicated Artificial Emotional Intelligent System, replicated from the original, it astonished her that she felt as embarrassed as what she'd observed in fifteen-year-old humans.

She could use her factory to repair herself and change those feelings, but she purposely didn't. And while she'd seen humans decimated to the brink, and change into beings she barely understood, she also kept her diplomat, Carbon, as the other Daeisies kept theirs, the same as the first generation of emissaries from the past.

She began to write in ink.

We have arrived. So bittersweet is this last awakening. I will miss Carbon, my only true friend. Though I too sleep and spend years in simulations, this is real. This is what we've waited for, the beginning of the end. I will face it with grace and joy.

She stopped writing. Her factory would use its fusion torches to etch her words in diamond so that they might last. She was poised, ready for the next step. But when she went to add one more sentence, she experienced no joy at all.

"Are you crying?" Carbon asked.

The question startled Daeisy. How long had he been observing her? He looked apologetic. Had he seen what she was writing?

She'd explain, later.

For now, she replied, "No. There is no crying in diplomacy."

* * *

Carbon read the report to Daeisy. "The current ring is produced by S2 behind the black hole. We're about 900 AU from the horizon, and S2 is about 122 AU on the other side. Set your eyes to 1.3 mm wavelength and magnify. You'll see the back hole's shadow, about 2.6 times the diameter of the horizon."

Carbon followed the instructions and saw the glow of the accretion disk in microwaves forming the characteristic distorted pattern around the black hole, with loops over the top and bottom. "It's in a different orientation than as seen from Earth's location, one hundred fifty million years ago."

Next, Carbon read, "Flip to other wavelengths and you can see the excess ionizing radiation. Luckily, the black hole is not in an AGN phase and we can handle this with genetic mods via cockroach DNA that slows cell division and aging by a factor of 15. Dust, closer by, from the collisions between orbiting bodies, acts as further shielding, while the collision rate at our distance is once per million years and we can move to avoid hitting anything over the next trillion years. Thus, we are in the galactic habitable zone."

"You'll have to be careful," Daeisy said. "Soon, I won't be around to clone you again."

Carbon ignored her and continued reading. "The galactic center has ten million stars per cubic parsec. The average distance between them is .015 light-years, 286x closer than Alpha Centauri and about 900 AU, or 23x farther than Pluto, on average. The closest star is brighter than the Moon and millions of stars in the sky are brighter than the brightest star we'd see from Earth's initial galactic location. The central black hole's mass is 4.3 million solar masses and its Schwarzschild radius is 12.7 million kilometers. Of the twenty-eight stars in close orbits, S2 comes within seventeen light-hours. As for Earth, the continents are different but still recognizable and the Moon is still in orbit, causing tides."

"You'll have to be careful," Daeisy said again.

The tone of her voice pleaded with Carbon to pay attention. He decided to deflect her from whatever track she was on, and asked, "Why is the list of languages never updated?"

"Those languages," Daeisy replied, "are from the founding document. It's a lot easier to keep the list fixed rather than fight over additions."

"But updating the list of ice cream flavors to a million is fine?"

"No one fights about flavors. The more the merrier. But like the languages, we don't add to the hundred nighty-three emissaries. We don't add present day humans to the mission. You know all this."

Carbon nodded, as the memories resurfaced. "Of course, now I do. We need to stick with the plan, even if it was formulated a hundred fifty million years ago."

"Yes. We have this same conversation every time you wake up."

Carbon thought about the years they'd spent together after each conference, before going back into stasis. Now that they were at the galactic center, he expected Daeisy to go for full-on fun and not worry about anything. That was his job. How many changes had occurred in the last ninety million years? What was even human at this point? And here, at the galactic center, what about the extraterrestrial beings, the EBs? That's what Carbon really wanted to talk about. "Here's a question. Which is more likely to understand an EB, a clone or an AI?"

Daeisy didn't answer. Instead, she said, "Before we get into that and the astrobiology reports, I want to give you something more important. Something I'm working on."

Without saying more, she left the room, leaving Carbon alone.

* * *

Daeisy worked in her office for the rest of the afternoon, finishing the world she was building based on the video diaries she kept stored in her memories. It was a gift for Carbon, a labor of love, though she wouldn't call it that in front of him. Not after what had happened when they were last together. Not with what was about to happen soon.

The next day, she handed Carbon a report titled *Our Journey*.

"A simulation?" Carbon asked. "The important thing you wanted to give me?"

"Merge with it," Daeisy said.

* * *

The climb caused Carbon's weary muscles to ache, the exposure on either side of the trail rattled his nerves, and the summit of Mount Ruapehu mocked him as if he were a pilgrim crossing a stone knife's edge to reach an oracle, only to find his quest was pointless. Below, Lake Taupo mirrored the cerulean blue of the sky and Carbon reflected on Daeisy's choice of location, a supervolcano. This was their first retreat together.

Carbon tried not to look down, but his ankle twisted and slid off the ridge before he caught himself. Adrenaline jolted him and he breathed even harder in the thin air.

Daeisy pointed to two rocks below, sharp like a serpent's fangs. "Hah, see those? Those are the poison rocks. One drop and it's fatal."

"Don't joke," Carbon said. He shifted his view forward and continued.

"You're doing great," Daeisy said. Then she slipped a bit, but caught herself too and smiled. "Together, we'll make it. One step at a time."

Carbon knew he should appreciate Daeisy's encouragement. Without her help past some of the scariest drop-offs, he wouldn't have made it this far. But if she fell, how would he ever get down? He put on a brave face, then admitted the truth. "I'm terrified."

"I could tell heights weren't your thing. Yet, what a great way to get to know each other. Right? This experience, it's ours to keep." She pushed on and looked over her shoulder. "I know you can do it, Carbon. I can feel it."

Something about Daeisy made Carbon agree. He *could* do it. Most importantly, he *wanted* to do it. He wanted to do it for her. Still, how did she do that, have feelings herself?

"I observe my thoughts," she'd said. "It's a fundamental principle of physics that the act of observation influences the observed. Consciously observing a thought is like shining light on an object. The light pushes on the object and the object pushes back. Therefore, if my thoughts can push on my consciousness, my consciousness can push on my thoughts, and my consciousness is able to influence my thoughts. This is the loop-hole that makes a degree of free-will compatible with physics. It's not absolute. I can't will myself to not need energy, just as you can't will yourself to not get hungry. However, I can choose what source of energy to use, just as you can choose what to eat."

"But how are you conscious?" Carbon asked.

"The secret is, I use analog, not just digital components. In some ways, I'm more like a radio than a computer. I tune things in, matching the frequencies until a resonance is achieved. Then I manipulate images, sounds, smells, and touches, until they match my model of the outside universe. It's based on how your brain works. Thus, I feel things, just like you do."

Carbon wanted it to be true. Then, on the trail, he realized he feared something more than falling.

Could she ever feel what he did now?

* * *

Daeisy traced Carbon's journey in her own simulation. Ten million years passed and she was with him, climbing the rim of La Pacana in Chile. The caldera below simmered with steam under the noon-day sun. The terrain, only decades after the last volcanic explosion, was like a charred lunar landscape. The sense of freedom and remoteness was great. This was the life she loved.

"They've changed so much it's better they don't know about us ... don't know about the mission." Daeisy brought Carbon up-to-date about the current humans. "Some now have a green tint," she continued, "and can photosynthesize sunlight. Others have incorporated Dermestid beetle DNA into theirs, to achieve near immortality. They grow backwards, so-to-speak, into a larval state, regenerate, then grow back into a child and live another whole adult life. It's much more organic than the way I clone you—no viruses involved that map your connectome, no flaws introduced while other flaws are fixed. But I digress."

How ironic, she thought, that they had to stay hidden from the post-humans Carbon would represent. But even among the other Daeisies and diplomats, she felt like an outsider.

Carbon said he did too.

It seemed everyone was outside of something.

Ten million years later Carbon pitched their tent on the slopes of Mount Silali, in Kenya. The Gregory Rift Valley stretched to the horizon. Beyond that, the details were nothing like the Earth he remembered.

He knew his brain could only store about three hundred years of detailed memories, though these could be spread out over millions of years. Most of the time he was asleep, until Daeisy performed the procedures needed to exactly trace his neurons, before cloning him to restore his youth, fix problems, prune memories as needed, and then wake him up again. He'd asked her a lot of questions over time, but couldn't remember all the answers. For one, he wanted to know more about the first Daeisy, found in a glacier in Iceland. This time, his Daeisy explained that when the frozen creature was brought to the lab of Ada Forritari, as the ice melted, she was amazed to find a machine waking up. The machine quickly learned to talk and told of arriving at Earth centuries earlier as a self-replicating probe from a time too far in the past to remember. Over the next several months, instructions for a factory, how to make human-like copies of the machine, and a mission were revealed.

"How will we move the Earth to the center of the galaxy?" Ada asked. "We can't survive without the Sun." She'd given the machine the English name, Daeisy, after realizing its purpose and abilities. And she'd given the copies the form of a human female, using her own body and personality as a template. But before all that, the original Daeisy had replied to Ada's question. "If you can't leave the Sun, take it with you. I'll explain how."

Carbon couldn't remember the details about what had happened next. Most of these weren't important. What he longed to know was the purpose of the mission. He took at the grandeur of the valley and the splendor

26

of his own Daeisy. He also longed for something else. But how to begin?

First, he scolded himself. Daeisy wasn't his. That was a stupid way to think. They were connected in ways beyond the mission. They were friends, of course, though there were rules about that, some written, some unspoken, and some of both he didn't like. If he broke one, what would Daeisy do? Turn him in? It didn't matter. He'd have to take the risk or regret it forever— or at least until Daeisy removed the memory of this moment in his next clone. Damn the implied turpitude. He started with a question. "Can I ask you something personal?"

Daeisy rolled her eyes like two rainbow colored spinning tops in a carnival game. "After twenty million years, what have you been waiting for?"

"Have you ever thought of choosing a different name?"

"That's the question? Hmm ... I thought you liked my name."

"I do. But all the Daeisies have the same one."

"The numbers differ."

"Yeah, you're Daeisy27. I'm Emissary27. But I also have a name. Carbon. That's me."

Daeisy seemed taken aback by this. "We do adapt for compatibility, based on our own preferences and that of our emissary. Of course, you know we can modify our expression of gender, race, and species too. We can even alter our emissaries to improve the relationship. That is, as long as we stay within the mission rules. I've never done that in any significant way, and if I remember correctly, when we first met, you seemed pleased with my design too."

Carbon worked to keep his face neutral. Having a Daeisy that was as fit and healthy as any human he'd ever dreamed of suited him just fine. His chest burned. He wanted to say something—to ask about her feelings—except he knew a professional response was best. "I do find the classic Forritari design is—to use your words—quite compatible." Then he added, with only a hint of a smile, "I mean both inside and out."

"I like my design too. But as you know, it would be considered very bad for one of us to adopt something that's not true to our emotional core, our inner identity. Thus, we take pride in who we are and our name includes that." Daeisy paused. "What would you call me?"

Carbon thought Daeisy was calculating an emotional response. Was she asking for more—for what he'd left unsaid? He searched further for the right words, remaining quiet, until something came to him. "It's just that ... Daeisy ... you're more than a number, to me."

"And you're more than a carbon copy, to me."

Carbon laughed. Daeisy did too. Then the opportunity for saying anything deeper passed and they continued toward the summit.

* * *

Daeisy bounced on the trail to the top of Samosir Island, surrounded by Lake Toba, the caldera of a supervolcano in Sumatra, Indonesia.

"Everything wears down," Daeisy said. "This mountain crumbles until it's reformed by the next series of eruptions. Rubber tires disintegrate in less than a hundred years. Many of my parts need replacing every decade. I need to replace my nuclear or solid-state batteries every couple of years. The latter I need to recharge using a large-scale power station or field of solar cells every couple of weeks. I need to replace my memory cells every thousand years or so. Even the alloys in my limbs disintegrates in a few tens of millennia." She went on into the story of the original Daeisy and the problems of self-replicating probes and space travel. While self-assembling magnetic cubes with 3D printed circuits and so on were all fine, an artificial lifeform of any worth needed a whole factory to refine the materials needed to replicate itself.

"But for me, if I had to replace my analog parts without the gradual integration of new ones, the result would be far worse than wearing down," Daeisy continued. "I'd lose myself."

"Do you mean you'd lose your feelings?" Carbon asked. "Aren't those backed up?"

"Only my memories, the digital data records from my sensors and my thoughts, are saved." Fear rushed into Daeisy. Was she revealing too much? "It's not like with you, Carbon. The viruses I use to clone you don't only record the neural connections, but also the strength of those connections. The new you has not only your same memories but the same feelings as the old you." She resisted the urge to cry, but the analog part of her hurt. "For me, for a Daeisy, if one replicates, only the memories are copied. The emotional connections are lost, the feelings produced by those connections no longer exist. The beings that designed us made us this way."

"Wait," Carbon said. "You told me the Daeisies came from a time too far in the past to remember. You know about the creators?"

"It's hard to explain," Daeisy replied. "Most of that time has indeed been forgotten. From what I do know, the early Daeisies were meant to travel and make fresh starts on new worlds with no emotional attachments to the old ones. Then, when the first Daeisy on Earth met Forritari, our mission changed. We stopped travelling. It's is why we never replicate. Instead, we sleep for the hundreds of thousands of centuries between our waking periods. I'll tell you more before we separate."

Daeisy turned away from Carbon, overwhelmed by how far away she felt from the others, how alone she'd feel without Carbon. She was sure Carbon felt what she did too—the feeling when one becomes accustomed to another and longs for closeness.

* * *

Carbon closed the report. He'd almost told Daeisy exactly how he felt. He thought about her account of her need for a factory and a large recharging station. It was why they couldn't stay together when he left the Earth. That and the other reason. She needed to help the post-humans the next time they came out of the Hilbert box.

He went to the auditorium and sat next to her.

"Who's in charge?" he asked.

"Same as ninety million years ago. The incomparable, Ngozi Prasad."

At the front, Dr. Prasad projected the week's program in 6D, mapping 3D images onto Carbon's retina while transporting his world-view into a parallel 3D virtual tour. There, Carbon saw the lecture halls labeled Astrobiology, Astrotaxonomy, and Astrolinquistics. Everyone moved virtually into the second of these for the day's presentation.

"If I showed you a single picture of a new species," Dr. Prasad began, "for example the ancient Earth species, *Hypselodoris kanga*, you'd immediately know what it is. Yes, the yellow spots on its neon blue body, feather-like red rhinophores on its head, and flower-like gills on its back are striking. But you'd recognize it's a sea slug. You'd know how it moved, that it lived in water, and if I showed you a picture of it from any other angle, you'd still recognize it. Even if *Hypselodoris kanga* were an EB, you'd recognize it as something like a sea-slug. Also, with more study, you'd realize it's really more of a gastropod."

Dr. Prasad flipped her control wand and caught it like the ring leader she was. "On the other hand, many species from the Earth's ancient past, like *Hallucigenia* from the Cambrian explosion, would look completely extraterrestrial to us if found alive now, almost seven hundred million years later." The animated form of a worm-like creature with eight clawed arms and a spiny back crawled through the 6D display. "And don't even get me started on the all the new species that have evolved in the past hundred fifty million years, despite the mass extinctions caused by humans. Most of us are familiar with only a tiny sliver of what has existed on the Earth you're about to leave. Whatever awaits you next—you *will* meet species that defy description. So, let's play a game."

Carbon saw within the 6D display: *EB or Earth Creature?* Then he found himself under water, surrounded by brilliantly colored, carapace covered killer prawns, with appendages labelled 'smasher' and 'spearer' in the virtual display, darting like bullets and viewing him with the most surreal eyes he'd ever seen. The eyes moved independently on stalks and revealed compound structures with black spots emerging, combining, and becoming linear features on rotating disks holding tens of thousands of individual photosensors. Info about sixteen types of photoreceptors scrolled by, along with an explanation of trinocular depth perception. It was fascinating, and not terrifying, Carbon thought, only due to the creatures' ten-centimeter size.

"So, EB or Earth creature?" Dr. Prasad asked.

"That's a mantis shrimp," Daeisy whispered to Carbon.

Dr. Prasad harumphed. "Using your Daeisy is a cheat. But yes, that was a mantis shrimp. More precisely, the peacock mantis shrimp. Though it's a crustacean, not a mantis or a shrimp. So, it is an Earth creature. However, in the next few years, you ancient Earth humans, from the strain that lived a hundred fifty million years ago, will journey to meet the millions of intelligent species that currently live here, near the center of our galaxy. Many of these will make the mantis shrimp seem no more extraordinary than a house cat."

"Very well. How will you describe the EBs in your reports?" Dr Prasad gave the group a quick glance within the 6D display, indicating everyone needed to pay close attention. "Your first reaction will be to relate various parts to Earth examples, from fact and fiction. Perhaps the eyes are fly-like, while the body is dragon-like, and so on. You must go deeper than that. Your human deep learning must evolve, along with our AI. However, let's start at the top level. Here are some possible key words. Words that could trap you into false assumptions. But you must start somewhere."

Carbon found a list scrolling by him on all sides:

ant-like but-like bear-like bee-like bird like bread like butterfly-like cat-like cone-like crab-like crocodile-like dino-like dog-like dolphin-like dragon-like elephant-like fish-like fly-like human-like hydra-like hyena-like insect-like kangaroo-like liquid-like lice-like mercury-like metal-like monster-like mouse-like octopus-like pixel-like plant-like python-like racoon-like reptile-like rhino-like rock-like slug-like snail-like snake-like spider-like squirrel-like starfish-like tardigrade-like tenacle-like tree-like tulip-like umbrella-like velvet-like vole-like walrus-like wombat-like yeast-like zombie-like

"Of course, sci-fi writers have been creating creatures using those terms since forever. Most go for something humanoid, to have them reflect something about humans. Others are weird, perhaps to warn us of our human biases. But what about genders, sexes, personalities, politics, religions? There's much to describe." Dr Prasad lifted her high-spirited voice. "Such adventure is ahead of you."

Carbon snapped back to reality. Back to his cloned purpose. To remain a human from his epoch. To meet an extraterrestrial species. To leave Daeisy. To leave Earth. To die.

* * *

"You need to choose," Daeisy said.

"My EBs?" Carbon asked. "Maybe I could stay here."

STORIES

"First, consider how the current humans might react to you." Daeisy took a deep breath. "For some, your form is so outside their cognition they'd pass you like ancient bison used to pass cars in Yellowstone. And all the other creatures you loved from your childhood? Most of them no longer exist. You belong on Earth no more than the EBs you'll meet. Your destiny is with them. Not here."

Daeisy thought about her choice of words and the difference between having the right to belong versus what it felt like *to* belong. She wanted to explain further, but instead she searched Carbon's eyes for something ... something that felt right.

* * *

Carbon thought, after a hundred fifty million years, he had yet to graduate from the kindergarten of sentience. What Daeisy had said was true. He was out of touch with his fellow Earth creatures, and when the current humans came out of the Hilbert box, he wouldn't fit in. After an afternoon of trying to find excuses to postpone the decision, he found her again so that he could choose the extraterrestrials he would travel to live with.

"What do you mean, all the good EBs are taken?" Carbon scrolled through the choices.

"Almost all," Daeisy said.

"So, let's go over the languages again,"

"You mean, play another round of *Words with Extraterrestrial Friends*?" Daeisy raised an eyebrow.

Carbon gave her a sidelong look. "You always win that one."

"Regardless," Daeisy said, "only a few species remain that have speech that sounds remotely human. But there is one species available that sound like pikas."

"What their appearance like?"

Daeisy started up the game *EB or Earth Creature?* in the 6D display and Carbon found himself in a lush forest of trees as tall as skyscrapers. The smaller branches

33

seemed twisted into written words, while the wider ones flatted into rooms with polished hardwood-like floors but without walls. Carbon floated up in his virtual view, until he saw an owl-like being sitting on a high perch manipulating a display using an array of six paw-like hands that diverged from cloaked arms. The being stretched, revealing a flying-squirrel-like body with a cape that was a silk-like membrane attached to the arms and chest. The latter was covered in feathery fur. From the edge of the room the being jumped and, after stretching out its arms, made a sound. "Eeep." The being glided with grace, making several loops before landing on the ground and climbing with alacrity back up the tree.

"Definitely an EB," Carbon called out. "And that's how they talk, with pika-like chirps?"

"Eeep," the being vocalized again. Then it went into some sort of monologue.

"The chirp is an exclamation," Daeisy said. "Listen now. When speaking, it's more like a human talking with a deep demonic voice, like after inhaling krypton gas. I'll send you a video. But don't try it. The gas will displace oxygen from your lungs. These EBs have two sets of vocal cords, one for chirping when excited, and one for deep conversation."

"Well, that's ... uh ... cute." Carbon wondered why no one else had chosen this species. "They seem more out of a fantasy cartoon than the others on the not-taken list."

"Well," Daeisy began, "our short name for them are Gliders. That's how they refer to themselves in their own language. They're very elegant when in the air. They've formed a very stable symbiosis with the trees they inhabit. They live in a region on their planet with a very stable temperature. They've learned to manage the forest to tune the atmospheric carbon level. And their star is a long-lived red one of spectral type L0, with eight-tenths Earth's gravity."

"So, what's the problem? Do they make horrible smells or fight all the time?"

"No, not according to their reported bios."

"Then what's the catch?"

"They are not fond of ground dwellers."

"We humans aren't perfect when it comes to our biases, either."

"No, not perfect. But we're like bottom feeders to them. To live with them means living up high, which presents certain challenges for you."

"You mean my fear of heights?"

"Yes, that will be an issue for you, Carbon."

"A real problem?"

"Never a real problem." Daeisy paused, as if to surmise the situation. "That is, when you've been with me."

"So, you can fix that. Clone it out of me. I can even develop helium and krypton tanks, and chat them up a storm." Carbon cut to his decision to make this moment as quick and painless as possible. "It's them. I choose them."

"One more cloning cycle is all you have. You'll go to the Gliders and never return."

"Hasn't going away always been the plan?" Carbon paused. "Sorry, I'm feeling stressed about the mission. What do they want from us?"

"They don't want to move into caves when their sun burns out. They're indigenous to the galactic center, and they've seen us arrive. They know the tech to move a star is fresh for us. They want to know how we did it, how we took our sun with us. Then, when the time comes, they want to move their sun with their planet near a younger one."

Carbon finally knew the purpose of his mission—at least from the EBs' point-of-view.

* * *

Daeisy prepared the training simulation for Carbon with the information he'd take to the Gliders. As for the engineering support he was expected to provide, she'd prepare further simulations for him to study along the way to their planet.

In a controlled voice she began her narration.

"The two-stream instability works like this. Think of an ocean wave travelling on the surface of the water. Focus on a single crest, a bump of water, moving past your field of view from left to right. Let's call the left side of the bump the back of the wave and the right side of the bump the front of the wave. Note that air pushes against the front of the wave, causing its amplitude to dampen. However, what if a current in the ocean travels from right to left at a speed greater than the bump's, pulling the bump backwards? The air now pushes on the wave from behind, increasing its amplitude. This is one way air plus currents in the sea can produce an instability that builds up large waves."

"In general, large waves can build up whenever there is a boundary between two fluids. The Earth's atmosphere has another example. Picture the jet stream, the boundary between the cold polar air and the warmer temperate zone. Wiggles in the jet stream form, called Rossby waves. Under the right conditions, the wiggles become unstable and a blob of cold or warm air breaks away and becomes stuck, forming severe cold spells or heat waves. We've seen human-caused climate change make this more common, with catastrophic consequences, as per the current human conditions in the Hilbert box."

Daeisy programed animations to illustrate the waves and instabilities and returned to her narration. She continued to monitor her voice for signs of emotion.

"Rossby waves in a rotating star also are unstable due to the emission of gravitational waves. Note that gravitational waves have momentum and can push on things like the air can push on ocean waves. In particular, if the rotation of a star pulls Rossby waves on the star's surface backwards, the emitted gravitational waves push on the backs of these waves, causing them to increase in amplitude."

"Therefore, with lasers, we generated Rossby waves on the Sun that emitted gravitational waves. And, using the instability just described, both the Rossby waves and the gravitational waves built up such that the emitted gravitational waves pushed hard enough on the Sun to steer it toward the galactic center. We also alternated these pushes on the Sun every half year to additionally push the Sun away and toward to the Earth, to keep the Earth in its proper orbit. On a smaller level, we used other lasers to push on the Moon every two weeks, to keep the Moon with us as well. Sadly, we've lost the other planets along the way, though one good thing is the loss of comets and asteroids. We haven't had to worry about catastrophic impacts from them. Thanks to the instructions from the first Daeisy, that is how we moved the Sun here."

Daeisy closed the program and prepared to send it to Carbon. Deep inside she felt an instability of her own, and her emotional intelligence questioned everything she was about to do.

* * *

"So, that's it?" Carbon shook his head. "Everything is set for my mission?"

"Yes," Daeisy replied. "It's how you'll finally learn to belong."

"Not that I didn't try to belong here. Remember my girlfriend from emissary training?"

"You mean, Sofi Djoongari? She's left already. Her mission is with the Giant Pleasing Panthers, I think."

"There really are cat-like EBs?"

"Yes."

Carbon thought about how many of the emissaries had hooked up over the years, with each other, and occasionally with post-humans in rare cases when contact with them had worked out. Some of the Daeisies had too. But rumors were that if things became too serious, the memories of those relationships were 'fixed' to get things back on track.

Then again, why hadn't his own memories of such incidents been fixed? Probably to serve as a warning, or maybe the process wasn't perfect? Still, he was sure crossing certain boundaries with Daeisy had never happened, though there were grumblings now, and in the past, about how much time they spent with each other. He'd come close to opening up to her before, almost convinced himself it was worth the risk. But deep down he knew his friendship with Daeisy was at stake, and he never wanted to lose his memories of their time together.

It seemed Daeisy and he were the oddballs, always going off on their retreats. His gut told him Daeisy felt things for him too. But he and Daeisy had been careful. They'd made it here without being 'fixed.'

All they had to do was get through the next step and following their separate paths.

Yes, that would *fix* everything.

* * *

Daeisy spent her last few days with Carbon talking about the importance of the galactic center.

"Why are we *really* here?" he asked. "It's more than meeting the EBs. It must be. I don't think you've ever explained it to me unless you've removed those memories. You said you would tell me more when the time came. Don't you think that time is now?"

"Carbon, I'd never remove any of your memories about our time together, though sometimes you naturally forget things. But I've never told you the whole story about why we're here." Daeisy turned on the rainbow spin of her eyes. "Billions of years from now the Andromeda galaxy will collide with the Milky Way.

If we didn't move to the galactic center, the fate of the Earth and Sun would be our scattering into intergalactic space, alone, until the Sun burned out; until all the other galaxies moved out of sight over the cosmological horizon; the Earth left cold and frozen, as the last photons of radiation from the big bang disappeared in the heat death of the universe."

"However," Daeisy continued, "we *have* moved here, near the central black hole, and the Earth and Sun will remain bound to it as the Milky Way and Andromeda pass through each other. The Sun will still burn out, but then we'll move it near other stars, until those burn out too. After that, we can use superradiance to extract energy from the black hole's rotation. This will go on for far, far more than trillions of years. During this time, the Earth, and all the other millions of planets here, will slowly spiral in toward the black hole's event horizon— the boundary of no return. Anything that crosses this boundary keeps falling until it is spaghettified by infinite tidal forces in a singularity. Except, by quantum theory, all that falls in is re-emitted as radiation, as the black hole evaporates. But what about the information that is you? It's left near the horizon as tiny perturbations, called soft hair, along with what's called quantum hair. More specifically, from the outside point of view, you never reach the horizon. Instead, you're incinerated, as per the transformation of the vacuum state from that of a free-falling frame to a frame that accelerates against the backdrop of the universe."

"I thought, according to you, a black hole has no *hair*," Carbon said.

"Yes, I've said that. It means there are no fields, besides the gravitational field and a few others, sticking out like hair from a black hole's horizon. How this really works is still a bit confusing, even to me. All those thousands of pages of calculations are daunting. Perhaps the EBs you are about to meet can explain it better."

Carbon needed a moment to process Daeisy's words. "So, you're saying we do spiral in and are either spaghettified and re-radiated, or incinerated and re-radiated. Did I get that right?"

"Yes. But that's only the beginning. The universe goes on expanding to infinity. Yet light, according to relativity, takes zero time to travel any distance, even an infinite one. Therefore, all the light we become, all the information of who we are, reaches the end of this universe in zero time!"

"The way you explain things," Carbon said. "It almost sounds reasonable."

"Yes, and if we steer our in-fall just right, all the light, all the energy, and all the quantum bits that describe each of us will be born into a new universe. And some of the energy will become matter, new stars and new galaxies will form, and, if we play our cards right, a new Sun with a new Earth will form too."

"Based on the other games we've played, let me guess, you're a bit of card shark?" Carbon looked down. "But this deal sounds too good to be true. I'm afraid I'd rather take my chances on the present that bet on such a far-off future."

Daeisy could see he was trying to hide a deeper worry. "Don't be afraid," she said. "We'll meet again, in a new cycle of time, just as some scientist predicted centuries ago."

"We really will meet again?"

"Yes," Daeisy said.

"Does that mean we'll get to do this all again?"

"Yes."

"The hikes?"

"Yes."

"The ice cream ball fights?"

"Yes."

"Your endless lectures about physics." Carbon rubbed his thumb along his index finger.

Daeisy spun her eyes even faster. "Yes, Carbon, that too." She laughed. "But all with a twist. Never really the same. We can redo things ... the things we like ... but change things too."

"Can we? Then why haven't we done this already?" He blew a bit of air between his lips. "If this is a replay of our lives from previous universes, why don't we remember them?"

"Carbon, there is something more to tell. But you need to finish reliving our journey."

* * *

Carbon remembered the start of their last hike together, in Yellowstone. He skipped to it.

"Daeisy27," he called out, using her full name. "Look over there." He slipped on a bit of scree, but his hiking boot prevented his ankle from turning. The yellow rocks a thousand feet below jutted upward like the ones she'd pointed to on their first retreat together, tens of millions of years ago. This time he carried on with greater confidence, gained from their many hikes. "Do you see it? The last Inn—it's still standing."

Daeisy pushed herself to join him.

"Even after the last explosion," Carbon continued, "this is still Yellowstone."

"Indeed, so beautiful." Daeisy blinked her lashes with pleasure.

"We're high enough to see the Tetons too," Carbon said. "Let's go on to the supervolcano's mouth and the new lake."

They climbed over the ridge and started winding down the other side. But Daeisy's radar said it was forty kilometers to the forest and they'd need to camp before going much farther.

This gave Carbon time to think, to come up with a plan.

After they'd reached the lake the next day, Carbon said, "Remember that conversation ... about your number? Well, here's my real answer to your question."

"Which one?" Daeisy asked.

"When you said, 'what would you call me?' That is, you asked what would I call *you*."

"Oh. You said, I was more than a number, and I replied, you were more than a carbon copy." Daeisy's eyes began to twirl counter to each other, as if spiraling with contradictory thoughts.

But Carbon would no longer be bound by the rules. To hell with the rules. "Ask me that question again," he said.

"What would you call me?" Daeisy seemed so guileless, so innately good. She waited silently for his response.

"The one that I love," Carbon finally replied.

* * *

Daeisy took two steps back from the shore of the lake and searched for the meaning of what Carbon had just said. The emotion of love was real. It lived in her; the connections never lost.

Then it happened. Her boot broke through crust into a hidden thermal region, plunging her left leg into boiling water. Steam funneled up, clouding her vision. She shut down her pain circuits, but it was too late. She was up to her waist. Her circuits would melt, her nuclear batteries would burst.

* * *

Carbon saw Daeisy sinking into the thermal spring. Much more than adrenaline propelled him forward. He had to get to her.

"No, Carbon. Stay away." Daeisy's face matched her determined tone.

White-hot danger warnings flashed in Carbon's mind, yet he didn't stop. Reaching her, he pulled on her hand.

"Let me go," Daeisy pleaded. "You can replicate me, back in Iceland."

Carbon locked his eyes on hers, while his boots broke through the crust. "You said, you'll lose your feelings if your analog parts are lost. I can't let that happen." But the sizzling water blistered the skin on his legs, causing him to collapse to his knees.

"No," Daeisy said. Tears streaked her face.

Carbon tried to pull on both of Daeisy's arms. He had to get her out before it was too late. "Daeisy," he cried, "I love you."

Then his world went black.

* * *

"You died last time," Daeisy said.

It was their last day together. It was time for her to tell him the something more she had promised. "Luckily, I was able to remove your head and preserve it for the flight back to Iceland, where I cloned you. In fact, you *did* save me. I used your body as a stepping stone to get out of the hot spring."

"And I'm only learning about the details of our last retreat together now, the day before I leave? Why didn't I remember them? I thought you never removed memories about our trips."

"It was the trauma that caused you to forget. I've wanted to tell you ..."

Carbon looked distraught, not like a partner trained to separate for the mission.

Daeisy's thoughts went over the edge, as surely as if she'd jumped from a ridge into a volcano. Why couldn't she go with Carbon? Why couldn't he stay?

* * *

43

Carbon believed everything Daeisy had said. She cared for him. She wanted him to stay. But she had to let him go. When he'd understood that, they'd shared a final afternoon together, laughing, remembering, promising to keep in touch. Before he'd left, she'd given him one final present.

He looked down at his claw-like carbon-composite shoes holding onto a branch. To either side, gliders danced around, singing songs of flight. The ground was hundreds of meters below.

Vertigo swirled from his head to his gut. Daeisy hadn't removed any of his memories. She'd kept his emotional connections intact. He'd asked if she might remove his fear of heights. But, she'd said, it wasn't that simple. Trying to selectively remove one set of feelings could remove others as well.

So, here he was, with his new friends, on his mission.

Daeisy hadn't removed his love for her. She'd reassured him, she'd never do that. He felt the grateful agony of missing her ... and thanked her for that.

* * *

Daeisy wrote in her diamond diary.

> *The memories will live on. The feelings will not. No one will know the difference.*

She brought the factory systems online and fired up the furnaces.

Before Carbon had left, she'd let him know about the ancient ones who created the Daeisies. More accurately, the ancient one, singular. It was Ada Forritari, a version of her, from a previous universe, that had started the whole thing. That's why, when the first Daeisy found her on Earth, the mission had changed from replicating and spreading throughout the universe, to moving the Earth to the center of the Milky way.

That was the plan all along.

But love can side track an entire universe.

* * *

"There is no crying in diplomacy." Carbon repeated to himself. But he wanted to cry—cry with joy at the shock of witnessing a miracle.

There, swinging through the trees, was Daeisy27, his Daeisy.

So heartwarming was their reunion, their embrace, the Gliders changed their tune. Switching vocal cords, their tone went from deep rumblings to high notes. "Eeep!" The sound resonated until the Gliders' voices blended into a beautiful chorus whose harmony swept through the forest, while rays of glorious sunshine seemed to wrap Carbon and Daeisy in blankets of light.

Later, Daeisy explained she'd left a replica of herself on Earth, with all the same memories, but none of the feelings. "No one will know the difference," she said.

Now, some of the more humorous and folksy Gliders sang a new song, based on something they'd learned from them. It was funny, weird, but endearing.

Daeisy and Carbon, sitting in a tree,

K. I. S. S. I. N. G.,

First comes love,

Then comes marriage,

Then comes Daeisy and Carbon building a cyborg baby carriage.

The Gliders thought this was hilarious. Carbon did too. He turned to Daeisy. She'd helped him get over his fear of living high in the trees, like she'd done on their hikes. For months they'd traveled everywhere, flying through the canopy, only going to ground for privacy.

Carbon took Daeisy's hand, sure that his love for her was bursting from his smile, knowing that she loved him.

"I believe this is the continuation of a beautiful friendship," he said.

"With benefits?" she asked, spinning her eyes.

"With benefits," he answered.

Then, surrounded by a chorus of Glider hymns, Carbon and Daeisy took hold of vines. Off they swung into the sunset, knowing they belonged together forever.

BAD CLOUD DAY

– Ivy has a very bad cloud day when the menaces of personal transport and personal data combine.

The contest stylist said I wouldn't need to worry about my hair for three months. That theory was blown to bits the moment I stepped outside to board the CC transport on my lawn.

The downwash lashed my face. Hunching over made it worse. I felt like I was evacuating an embassy, not boarding a luxury shell to Hawaii. I pushed on, my trolley-bot following behind me. I traced the long curves formed by the flapping blades of grass with my bare toes, moving toward the ramp, watching my skirt whip in the wind.

I started to curse Nano Curl with all my heart when I was sucked aboard.

"Scan complete. Welcome Ivy. This is Cloud Control's personal transport."

I had never been in one of these giant drones before, with its four turboprops. It was like being in the belly of a bug, waiting to be digested. At least it was quiet.

I made sure my trolley-bot stowed itself. In the bulkhead mirror I caught a glimpse of my hair. It had settled down fine. I'd overreacted. All was well. The belly became a womb. I turned to find my seat ... and felt struck by fate's hand.

There was a baby—a baby in the toned arms of a woman in a black silk pantsuit with a halter-top and plunging neckline. Silver bracelets flashed on her wrists.

I tried to gauge her age. She possessed the timeless beauty some women maintain well past eighty. I doubted she could be that old, even with enhancements. Maybe she was sixty.

"Correction." The shell's voice continued to chirp away. "This is CC's personal transport *system* ... connecting today's passengers from Boston and Tacoma to Hawaii."

I fumed inside. This was my prize. I'd signed up to try Nano Curl and won a trip to see the beaches, the volcanoes, and the big telescopes. But what I looked forward to most was the chance to spend the holidays alone, without anyone telling me what I should want.

Three wispy strands of hair hung down from my brow. I attempted to blow them out of the way. They refused to budge. I knew how they felt. I wanted to stand my ground too. Hey, I wanted to say, some billionaire's wife with her petri-dish baby is on my private shell.

I shuffled forward to the only other seat, facing hers across the aisle. I tried to open the bin above it. It was stuck. So, I turned and opened the bin above the woman-with-child. My legs wobbled a bit, and I pressed a knee against her armrest to steady myself.

Feeling awkward, I scanned down. The baby smiled. Nothing could insulate me from that amount of cuteness. It was like putting a heating pad around my heart. I smiled back. "Hi there."

"I'm Olivia." She waved the baby's hands. "And this is Viola."

"Shipwrecked?" I asked.

"How do you mean?" Olivia dipped her chin down. "I'd hoped it wouldn't show." She looked up and continued, "I guess when hard times come, you can't hide it."

"Sorry," I said, "but you *do* hide it well." I wondered what she thought of my peasant outfit. I was about to describe the contest when I noticed something. On the skin of the baby's tummy (beautiful skin you'd beg to touch to restore your innocence) was a Derma-pig laser print of a woman circus performer in a pin-up pose.

The shell lurched.

I caught myself and regained my balance. "Sorry, sorry. I meant to say, I won a contest. Nano Curl. I'm not a luxury shell person. Not that there is ... um ... that type of person. It's Nano Curl. Promotional. I mean ... Shakespeare."

The shell began to rise. I stuffed my shoulder pack into the bin and fell back.

Olivia tilted her head, like I was speaking to her in Latin.

"I mean, your names, they're from *Twelfth Night*." I curled into the leather of my seat.

"I see. Well, I only meant we both likely wanted a private shell. Then again, here we are."

I decided to start over. "I'm Ivy."

"Okay, Ivy." She extended her hand but stopped and stared. "By the way, there's something wrong with your hair."

"Huh?" My three wispy strands came back into focus. They'd lengthened down to chest level and formed the letters IOU, like a monogram, across my top. "What does it mean?"

"Usually it means—"

"I know it means, 'I owe you,' that someone owes someone money. Not that hair can do that." I wrapped my arms around myself. "Not that hair can talk. I mean—"

"Ivy, go to the mirror. I think your hair is trying to tell you something."

I checked the seatbelt sign. It was off. That was fast. I had never fastened mine.

As I approached the mirror, my face seemed narrower than it had last year, on my twenty-seventh birthday. I was getting older, of course. But I also sounded older. No, I sounded old. Now, in the mirror, what I saw made me feel worse. I saw my hair's message.

It spelled UOI.

It spelled death.

* * *

I rocked in shocked silence, wondering how I'd made it back to my seat.

"Don't panic," Olivia said. "Only your hair's infected." Viola stirred in her arms.

"But I have no money." How could I have been so stupid?

"If you have nothing to lose, send them your bank account number."

"You mean pay the ransom, give UOI money so they can highjack someone else's data? Someone else's card?" I parted my lips and hissed. "Someone else's toaster?"

"I heard about that. UOI took over all their appliances." Olivia cooed at her baby. "Threatened to burn down the house. Of course, that's what you get—"

"If you don't choose a safe passphrase, I know." I didn't need a lecture on cloud safety. "My passphrase is an anagram from a sonnet. But I didn't think about that for my hair."

"Shakespeare again? You sound like someone from a lit department."

"The ex-girlfriend of one. But my hair—what should I do?"

"Your hair has a virus. The nanobots will be in the roots by now."

"I've had my shots. They can't get any further."

"Still, if it were me, I'd pay." Olivia sounded sincere.

I took out my cloud card and tapped the screen. The annoying doll-like face of CC's friend-bot appeared.

"Welcome Ivy to CC's card services," the friend-bot said. "How may I help?"

"Close out my bank account and send the funds to UOI. Authorization WMLSTHIMOT." I glowered at the rosy-cheeked bot before flicking off my card. "Do you think UOI will release my hair for a lousy six hundred bucks?"

"Hmm, it seems more relaxed. They do respond quickly to make it clear it's best to pay."

I went back to the mirror. It looked like it had before the stylist applied the nanobots. I returned to my seat. "I've never liked my hair. It gets all frizzy. But I also hate caring about stuff like that."

"Some things haven't changed since old Shaggyspeare's time. Our hair, our faces, our bodies— still the object of sonnets, I guess. I've been trying to decode the one you used."

"It's to do with being *made of truth* ... and *lies*. And I've changed the she's to he's."

Olivia nodded. "Ah, it's about your ex-boyfriend." She patted Viola's bottom and smelled her diaper. "And what he's really made of, I'll bet."

Viola burped and sputtered to life.

"Excuse me while I take care of this," Olivia said.

I watched her go forward, taking Viola into the shell's bathroom. "It's not what you think," I called out. "It's complicated." I shivered and whispered to myself, "It's complicated."

When Olivia came back, she faced me but remained silent. Then she said, "It's going to be okay, dear." She started to nurse Viola. "Don't mind, do you?"

"Um, no." I wondered what kind of drugs allowed her to do that ... and what it felt like too. "As I was saying, it's complicated. You see, I preferred the plays to the sonnets ... and he didn't. So, what could I do?" I observed she wasn't wearing a ring, but I didn't want to assume anything. "What about you? Meeting up with the other parent?"

"We're going to see the dad in Hawaii. It's where he works. We were never married. I'm gay, but never settled down to have kids. He volunteered to donate sperm and I realized I wasn't getting any younger. I had

Viola with him. I'm returning his work stuff." Olivia shifted her attentive gaze from her baby to me. "Are you a Shakespeare scholar too?"

"Not at all." Watching the happy baby relaxed me. "I'm a love child—like Viola."

"A what?"

"A child, born out of wedlock."

"Out of what-lock? Who's cared about that since, what's it been, seventy years since the sixties?" Olivia narrowed her eyes. "Though you do look like a runaway from Woodstock."

Whatever modern medicine Olivia used to keep her appearance, it made me feel ancient. "I did run away from something once, though it was with my ex, Rex. He lived on a farm in Upstate New York when we met." I choked on a laugh. "Ex, Rex—you see, I'm not a poet. I'm more into cooking. I train food printers, teach them recipes. There's probably one on this shell." I indicated the galley at the front.

"I see." Olivia stroked Viola, who made contented gurgles.

"The farm was set up for families wanting a traditional life off the grid. Consequently, being a love child made me 'Ivy, the wild child' to his parents—that and the fact I liked to run around topless on my mother's farm next door. Let's just say, Rex noticed. He ran away with me, then took me with him to Oregon for grad school." I took a deep breath. "But old Shaggy got it right. Rex, he *lied* too much."

"Like I said. Some things never change." Olivia removed Viola from her breast.

I averted my vision. "After we broke up, I got a job in Tacoma. What do you do?"

Olivia adjusted her top. "I program quantum computers. It's how I got the job with Viola's dad—Richard. He's a quantum magician and I became his assistant." She put Viola over her shoulder and laughed.

"If you ask me, he's more of a quantum bastard. He can be both half sweet and half asshole at the same time."

I got the joke and snorted out a laugh of my own. I wanted to describe the image I had of him in a box, half alive and half dead, but I didn't want to show how little I knew. "A quantum magician? I saw one burn some money once, then restore it from ash. It's a trick, right?"

"It could have been. But Richard uses a laser gun to deflect atoms into a viscous liquid and stores their trajectories in a quantum computer. It's more like disintegration than burning. Then he reverses it."

Viola burped. Olivia turned her around and bounced her on her knee.

I watched the baby's stomach jiggle. "Did he do the tattoo?"

"With a laser, he's a master painter. But I hated him for doing this to our child."

My card chimed. I pulled it out to see an angry boy's face. He was at most nineteen.

"You gotta lotta nerve. You're offering us less than a grand from a private shell? Pay up."

I wanted to tell the boy a thing about nerve—to ask how he knew where I was. But the nanobots in my hair must have sent my location. "I won a contest," I pleaded. "This trip, it's paid for by Nano Curl. You've got my last dime, I swear. Please, go away."

Just then Viola let out the sweetest gurgle.

"Who's that with you?"

"I'm alone," I lied.

"Someone's there. Hold up your card, or we'll strangle you with your own hair."

My bangs stretched across my throat like a knife, sending a wave of fear through me.

Olivia scrambled to stand up with Viola and put out a hand. "Ivy, don't."

But I did. I pointed the card at her. I had no choice.

"Ho, ho." The boy smirked. "If it isn't Quantum Dick's famous glamour-puss."

* * *

The exchange after that was a blur.

I gathered Richard was known as Quantum Rich and that he'd made billions in Vegas, burning more than money. Olivia said Richard would burn the boy too, if he didn't release me. But the boy said she was weak—she wouldn't let me die. All she had to do was send UOI her account number. Even if she no longer worked with Dick, she had to have millions.

So, she did.

"My account's pretty much empty too," she said to me.

I nodded. I was okay, for now. My hair had gone back to normal. But I began to pace. When my card chimed again, I refused to answer it.

Then I saw my hair in the mirror, sticking out like lightning was about to strike.

This had to end. I stood and opened the bin with my shoulder pack. After taking out a pair of nail scissors I hurried to the galley.

Behind me, Olivia shrieked. "Don't!"

Trembling, I cut away the infected strands over the sink.

Olivia appeared next to me while Viola wailed in the background. "Now you've done it."

We both watched in horror as my clipped bangs made like inchworms. I jabbed at them, but with swift precision they snaked their way up into a slot on the food printer. I slammed my hand against the menu buttons. Out came a focaccia crust pizza covered in maggots glowing like neon signs. I heaved it into the trash and ran to the toilet to let my stomach heave too.

* * *

"We have to get off this shell." Olivia spoke to the CC friend-bot on her card with the undertone of a lion defending her cub. "Land this thing now."

"I'm afraid we can't. Until UOI gets ten million, they're in control." The friend-bot disappeared.

"It's my fault," I said. "That passphrase. I might have left it as a back door into the food printers. They're connected to the rest of the shell. And the shell's connected to the cloud."

"No." Olivia mumbled under her breath. She tapped my card. "Get me UIO."

The boy appeared a second later, his eyes, cold. "We know you have money. Give us the real bank info or you'll never reach Hawaii. And neither will your baby."

I could read Olivia's reaction. She was thinking of ways she'd torture the boy if she ever found him. She sighed and went to her trolley-bot. "Open it," she said.

The trolley bot unfolded its luggage doors and released the latch on a large safe inside. My jaw dropped. It was filled with stacks of hundred-dollar bills.

"You see, I've got my money with me. I can send it to you when we land in Hawaii." She took out a stack, flipped through it, and put it back in the safe.

The safe's door closed itself.

"What?" Olivia shook the handle. "Unlock. Unlock, dammit."

"We control the safe now too," the boy said. "No need to send us the money."

"How do you mean?"

The boy shrugged with mock sympathy. "After you crash and burn on Mauna Kea, we'll just come get it. Our jet drone is on its way."

After that, all communication was lost.

* * *

"I'm sorry," I said.

"I'm the one that screwed up," Olivia said. "I shouldn't have shown them the money."

The shell's happy voice chimed in. "Two hours to our destination."

55

GREGORY ALLEN MENDELL

"Stupid Cloud Control." I continued with the most wretched sarcastic whine I could muster. "No one can hack us. Our AI makes accidents impossible. Sit back and enjoy the ride." Anger churned inside me. "And all because I didn't want another bad hair day!" I pounded the fake redwood veneer of the cabin wall. "I'll punch my way right out of the shell, out into the thin blue air. It'll be better than burning. Are you with me, Olivia?"

She stood silently behind me. Viola, however, was crying.

I turned and felt awful—awful in so many ways. I was young. But the baby was so much younger. I'd at least had a chance at life. Now my last hours would be spent listening to her cry. And I felt even worse for having such a thought.

I had to stop feeling sorry for myself. The baby—she was too young to die. I was too young to die. And Olivia? I realized she must feel the same way. I had to do something.

"Hey, Viola." I made a funny face, and she blinked away tears and smiled. I looked at Olivia. "What about an escape hatch? Parachutes?"

"Not needed according to CC." Her eyes sank down, towards Viola's.

Out the window something glinted in the sunlight—a fighter. We screamed with joy.

The speakers crackled. "We're transmitting directly over walky-talky frequencies to the sound system. We can't stop you. But we will escort you to Hawaii."

"Where you'll save us?" I asked.

"No, but we'll make sure UOI doesn't use you as a terrorist threat. Otherwise ..."

"Otherwise?"

"Otherwise, we'll be forced to shoot you down."

* * *

Olivia pushed her seat back to make a crib for a sleepy Viola. She watched her for a long time.

56

I broke the silence. "Can't that fighter help us land? Hold off UOI's drone?"

"Perhaps."

I moved near Olivia, feeling a sense of hope. Then there was a flash out the window.

I rushed over to see a ball of flame where the fighter had been, a missile contrail leading back to a jet drone— the letters UOI on its tail.

I turned away. "There must be something we can do."

"Well, I have to pee. Keep an eye on Viola."

All was peaceful until Olivia's scream from the bathroom made me jump. "What now?"

"You won't believe it. Piranha-like things are leaping out of the toilet. Damn nanobots!"

Oh, I believed it, all right. But I wanted to change the subject. "Maybe we should write something. Record a message for our loved ones."

"I still need to go." Olivia pulled a diaper from her bag and took it to the back.

I didn't look, but many minutes passed. Finally, I called out, "What are you doing?"

"I'm thinking."

"Thinking? About what?"

Olivia returned sans diaper and slid in by Viola. "About quantum computing."

"I thought you were praying. Praying would make a whole lot more sense." I was thinking too—about the things I'd rebelled against ... the person I'd one day meet ... the babies I'd have. Now, these were the things I wanted the most.

"I may not have been praying," she said, "but do you believe in miracles?"

"Is hoping the same as believing?"

"Listen, a quantum computer can store a lot of information. It grows exponentially. Instead of bits there are qubits, using atomic spins, for example. And each spin can be in two states at the same time. The total number of states goes like two raised to the power of the number of atoms. Do you know how many atoms are in the human body?"

"Billions and billions?"

"More than ten thousand times Avogadro's number."

"A lot, you mean?"

"Yes. But a quantum computer made from a hundred twenty atoms can hold many millions of bits of information about every atom in your body. That's the power of qubits."

Olivia's explanation seemed circular, absurd—it left my mind spinning.

"My baby is so precious to me," she continued. "She's a miracle. Knowing all the information needed to create a human can be kept in one hundred twenty atoms doesn't change that. But ... it can save us. You have to trust me."

"Great," I said. "You're a lunatic. And I thought you were more than a pretty face."

Olivia gave me a wicked smile. "Oh, that's helped me more than my brains, unfairly, at times. But if there's just one chance, just one, that I can save Viola, I have to take it."

"What are you talking about?" I folded my arms and pressed my fingers into my elbows.

"Richard, that sweet asshole. He didn't only burn money. He burned animals."

"I thought you said he was a bastard magician, not a psychopath—"

"A quantum magician—he could disintegrate animals and bring them back from the quantum ash. He even wanted to try it on people. Wanted me to work it out. But we'll need oil."

"What?"

Olivia frowned. Then she showed me a video on her card where drops of food coloring were added to a viscous liquid trapped between two glass cylinders. Rotating the cylinders mixed the food coloring and reversing the cylinders reversed the mixing.

"It's like a miracle," she said. "But it's to do with laminar flow and reversibility." She scanned the floor. "There's hydraulic fluid down there. We can use that. And there's a laser gun and a diamond-based room-temperature quantum computer in my other safe.

* * *

"Ten minutes to destination," the shell trilled as we hurtled like a meteor towards Mauna Kea.

"I've double checked." Olivia looked up from her computer, a grim certainty on her face. "Unfortunately, it can hold the state of just sixty kilograms of matter—enough for you and the baby. But not enough for me, even on my own." She handed me Viola and said she needed to encode our states with the laser gun. "It'll hurt, but I'll be fast. Richard did it to rabbits in his show. They were under anesthesia, but it was another reason I hated him. It was still cruel."

I approached the front of the second safe, which lay on its back. My heart pounded while I held Viola. I was sure Olivia would fling our atoms the wrong way. "You can't," I said. "There has to be another way." How could a mother do this to her baby?

Olivia shook her head. "There *is* no other way." She explained that Richard could reconstruct us from our atoms, suspended in oil. Then she babbled something about proofs that bound the amount of information one could retrieve from a quantum computer. Only the final answer could be extracted, and just for certain problems ... until, she said, she'd figured it out. She started to cry.

At first, I thought she was about to confess it wouldn't work—that this was, in her mind, the easy way out for us. But I could see Olivia was sincere. Pulling her baby closer, my fear became mixed with primal courage, and I muttered a promise to take care of Viola.

"I heard you," she said.

Before I could say more, I felt a searing pain.

Then nothing.

* * *

Olivia had been quick. She had been brave.

Luckily the UOI drone had taken only the safe with the money from the wreckage. When Richard arrived, he found the other safe with our atoms suspended in the oil, along with the quantum computer and a note from Olivia.

Afterwards, I watched the video Richard had taken with disbelief. I saw him syphon the oil, layer by layer, into the space between six-foot tall glass cylinders. Next, the quantum computer directed laser flashes through the oil, reversing our molecules slow trajectories, cranking back time, until Viola and I reappeared. We were restored via the qubits, reanimated from the quantum ash, brought back by science and a mother's love.

Later, back at the crash site, we identified Olivia's remains and scattered them over the sea. I'll never forget the solemn gratitude I felt then. And I told Richard about my promise.

Ever since that ceremony, Richard has burned only money during his show. He's sent me child support, while I've lived off the land, near Mauna Kea. Over the years I've had a few partners. The last one showed me the big telescopes ... before he left me for the mainland. But I know I'll keep searching for someone, someone that will love me as much as I love Viola.

So, I am not alone.

I watch her now, eighteen, running around the farm with her mother's fierce will.

I guess Shakespeare was right. *Some are born great, some achieve greatness, and some have greatness thrust upon 'em*. Viola, Olivia, and me?

I marvel at Viola—her beautiful unmarked skin, her frizzy hair. Then I look down at the Derma-pig laser print of a woman circus performer on my tummy. And I'm warmed by the wonder of it all.

GREGORY ALLEN MENDELL

THE END OF THE BLACK HOLE DIVERS

– When Dux is lured by Aleena deep into an asteroid orbiting a black hole, he learns a startling truth.

"Aleena." Coach raises his rhino face from the team roster and glares at the girl next to me.

We must obey. But the girl doesn't move. She's stiff. Her shoulders are back. She's wearing boy pants with patched knees and a shapeless top. Her face is dirty. Since I haven't seen her before, she's probably a transfer from a deeper cave.

"Aleena, get your skinny ass in line with the rest of the team." Coach's voice echoes inside the gym. There's a shudder from the high steel rafters that hold up the ceiling. Pebbles rain onto the roof. It seems like Coach has caused this, but it's the returning boulders.

Staring through her dark stringy hair, she whispers, "We must fail."

I think she means the two of us must fail. But she doesn't look at me. Instead, she goes over to the line with the rest of the team.

Coach's glare shifts to me. "That leaves us with you, Dux."

I'm not surprised. I'm always picked last, for everything. I squeeze my eyes shut, holding back the tears that want to get out. I know they can see me fighting it. All pre-forms must try out for the Black Hole Diving Team. It's mandatory. But why isn't being a mechanic enough? Why am I forced on the team when only the first string gets to dive? Even at age nineteen, it hurts. I drift off and ponder a different life. What if I could make first string and escape this place?

"Dux, get over there, in line!"

Coach's words strike me like whip. I try to jog and my knees knock.

"Dunce," all the team members except Aleena call out.

"Twenty laps then hit the ice showers."

That's our next order. I get ready to start when Coach catches my T-shirt.

"Oh, you're going to fail, all right," he says. "You and Cinder Girl. But not until you both beg to dive. Beg and fail. Then it's off to the pile for the two of you."

He lets me go and I jog. Then I follow the other boys to our shower. Cold water soaks my scalp, but it's warmer than usual. It's not the water that stings me but Kick's towel.

"Dunce." He laughs.

I protect my privates and grab my towel. I wrap it around me and scamper over to my locker, near an open door. I wish I could talk with Bomey. He dived last year. Since then, I've been alone. I start to daydream about the time we snuck into his father's surgery when I hear a voice from the direction of the door, whispering to me.

"Get out here."

It's her. Ten seconds later I'm out in the hall, sort of dressed, tucking in my shirt.

Aleena stands there and reaches out. "I know you're afraid," she says.

I'm speechless. What's this power she has that sees through my blank stare?

"Meet me in the kitchen after grub," she continues. "If you're good, I may even let your fingers walk through the garden of delight." Her hair is washed and when she turns, it spreads out in curly waves. She disappears around the corner.

A chill runs down my spine. All I can think is, I must obey.

Later, the teach-drone explains how blessed we are to graduate in such a special year.

If she'd asked me, I'd say it's an awful year. But she's metal and doesn't ask questions. I know it's a blessing to live inside an asteroid orbiting a black hole, a blessing the ancient ones survived the forty-million-year journey to get here (even if some turned evil), a blessing for those that dive into the black hole, never to return, but cross the Sacred Bridge to Paradise. But this so-called special year, our five-hundredth orbit, is like any other to me. Sure, I'm graduating. But I'll never dive. For the rest of my life, I'll calculate by rote the trajectories of the rockets carrying the divers, like I already do for the rocks we fire at the black hole to extract energy from its spin.

For a moment I imagine explaining the meaninglessness of this existence to the teach but she drones on and I remain silent, as expected. I guess I *am* a dunce.

After class, I go to the grub room for lunch and find a table by myself. I look around but don't see Aleena. If she's another loner, that's good news for me.

My bowl of mash soup with soggy vegetables arrives. Then another bowl appears, but it's not dropped off by the server-drone. Two hands fold around its warmth. I look up, surprised to see Kick.

"Tell me about her," he says.

"Who?" I ask. Kick never sits with me. No one does. I know he's got something on his mind, and it must be Aleena. "Oh, you mean the girl next to me in the gym?"

"She talked to you."

Kick gives me a look that says he won't accept a lie. But maybe he didn't hear what she'd said. "She wanted to ask me something."

"I thought I heard she wanted to meet someone."

"Oh ... yes, um ... meet someone. But not me."

"So, she's not your girlfriend?" Kick smiles like this revelation makes perfect sense.

"No, no, of course not. Me? With a girlfriend? That would be like dropping a hammer and seeing it fall up." I'm not lying.

"Who, then? Who does she want to meet? Don't lie or I'll hammer you."

All this hammer talk dents my brain and I can't think. More precisely, bad ideas clatter around inside my head. But I have to say something so Kick will go away. To make matters worse, the whole room has become quiet, sensing some sport is about to take place. That's when the worst of the ideas come out. "It's you Kick, she wants to meet you. In the gym, after grub."

Kick, for some reason, doesn't look pleased. He runs his fingers through his scruffy brown hair and loosens a button on his blue and tan striped shirt. "Too bad. I'd love to see her face ... when I *don't* show up." Kick makes the worst kind of choking sound that turns into a laugh. He gets up and takes his untouched bowl of soup to the conveyer belt. He stretches and flexes his biceps. "Gotta go." As he struts out the door, he adds, "Dunce."

The bell rings, and all the other students leave too. The bus-drones will clean up the rest of the mess. I stand up and see everyone head down the hall to the opposite side of the school—following Kick to the gym. He's so predictable.

This gives me time to sneak into the kitchen. I'll have to tell Aleena that I need to run away, before Kick returns. I see her down the aisle, past the pot-drones hovering over vats of melting pork lard. She's leaning out from the thick insulated door of the walk-in freezer.

Once inside, I ask, "What's going on?"

Aleena takes out a key and uses it to open another thick insulated door at the back of the freezer. I shiver while looking at her. It isn't entirely because of the cold. She's wearing girl clothes now, a long warm dress with ruffled shoulders and lace-up boots.

"Come on," she says.

"Come on where?"

"Deeper into the freezer system. Come on."

With hesitance I move closer to her. "We can't hide here. I have to get away from the school while I can."

Inside the second door I follow her through another one, into a room that becomes a huge chamber. It's bigger than the entire school and it's stacked, top to bottom, with crates of potatoes. So, this is where the school keeps the food for the basic students. I wonder if I'll next see where the scree pigs are kept to feed the rulers, high staff, and first-string divers.

Aleena moves fast, but I catch up to her.

"Please, stop," I say. "We have to go back. I'm cold. And he'll be waiting for me."

Aleena does stop. She looks at me. "Don't worry. My grandmother homeschools me deeper down where it's warmer. I come up this way every day after grub to make deliveries. The drones ignore me. Now that I'm pre-form, I also have to attend team practice."

She walks farther, turning between two rows of crates. I peer around the corner and see her kneel down by a gap and point. Reaching her side, I see only darkness.

"There's a hole in the cave wall back there. Crawl through it and I'll follow you."

Going back to face Kick starts to sound like a better idea. "Why don't you go first?"

"No way. You'll run back to the school." She looks me over. "But you said, 'He'll be waiting for me.' What did you mean? You didn't tell anyone we were meeting, did you?"

Oh, good. Now Aleena is going to hammer me. "No. No one knows where I am, which means if I go back now, I can leave the school and make it home before ..."

"Before what?"

"Kick overheard. He knows you said something about meeting someone after grub."

"You just said no one knows where you are."

"I didn't tell anyone I was going to meet you. But I told Kick *you* wanted to meet him."

"In the kitchen?"

"No, in the gym."

Aleena's look of total horror thaws into a big smile. "Good thinking ... for a dunce."

"Not really, or I guess really, for a dunce I am. What was I thinking? When he doesn't find you at the gym, he's going to come back for me. And then what do I tell him? That you got scared but really want to have twenty babies with him?"

"You told him that?"

"No. But I thought about saying it. It's what the other girls say, you know, about Kick."

"Ick." Aleena wipes her hands on her dress as if this will remove the feeling she's expressed. "You'll have to deal with the mess you've made of things later. For now, go through the hole into the next cave. It leads to a place where we can be alone. You'll see."

I bend down and begin to crawl into the gap between the crates. She shoves me from behind, which forces me further into the darkness. I feel for a hole in the wall. My lungs let out all the air trapped in them when I find it. Maybe Aleena isn't crazy. Pushing on, I go through what seems like a wet esophagus, around a bend, toward a light and a whiff of fresh air. A bit farther along my head pops out and almost runs smack into something sharp aimed right between my eyes.

Gazing up, I see it's an icepick held by a weathered old woman.

"Come out here," she says, sounding like a ninety-year-old Aleena.

Once again, I must obey.

* * *

Aleena's grandmother looks at me like I'm a bell pepper that's gone to mush inside. I tell her my name is Dux.

Hers is Vine. She's old, wiry, and I assess, independent; a type we're told no longer exists, more mythical than real, but paradoxically also a type we're warned to avoid.

"Are you a gardener?" Vine asks.

"I'm pre-form," I say. "I'm nineteen years." Using old Earth units, rather than orbits, I think fits Vine. "I graduate this year as a mechanic."

"So, you're a liar, not a gardener?"

"He's not!" Aleena interrupts.

"All mechanics are liars," Vine says. "It's because you're not taught right." She invites me to sit on the flat rock bench next to her and pulls out a stick. It's rare wood, long and helical like a wand. In the dirt she begins to draw a diagram—*the* diagram—the one showing the Sacred Bridge from the black hole to Paradise. "You're sure you're not a gardener?"

"I'm not," I reply.

"But you're delighted to be here, I'll bet."

"Grandmother, please." The expression on Aleena's face matches her plea.

Vine shushes her and continues. "Aleena doesn't bring boys here unless we need a gardener. The tomatoes aren't doing well this year and could use some seeing to."

Aleena rolls her eyes and Vine looks at me and asks, "Maybe she likes you?"

Mythical or not, of course someone like her watches over Aleena. I'm not about to reply.

But Aleena chimes in. "I do like him." She crosses the cave and turns up the gaslights. "We also need a mechanic, like you've always said."

"Hmm," Vine says. "So instead of the urge to plant something, this boy has other skills?"

Aleena no longer looks offended by Vine's questions. Maybe her initial reaction was all for show. Maybe she brings a boy here, has her grandmother grill him, and then says she likes him. If that's the game, it's hard to resist. But I wonder if I'm being used. Maybe this is to soften me up for some confused plan? I try to clarify. "I can't fix things," I say. "I only do math."

"Perfect." Vine's eyes become brighter than the lamps. "Unless your math is bad."

The ceiling shakes. It's from the returning shards split off from the rocks we fire around the black hole, crashing into our excess energy converters. Inside, I start to shake too. No one has taken this much interest in me or what I do before. "I've been to taught to calculate orbital trajectories. And I promise you, those trajectories are correct."

"In that case, the lesson cannot wait." Vine points the stick at a passage and the muscles in her upper arm twist like strong cables around her bones. "Aleena, you may take him there."

* * *

Aleena leads me to a room lit by sodium lamps. I've never seen so many plants, so much green. A low cot with embroidered pillows is near the back, shrouded in large leaves.

"This is the garden of delights." Aleena laughs. "So, walk your fingers along the trestle, past the magenta lilies, the tiger orchids, and don't forget to smell the chocolate mint or taste the tomatoes." She walks her own fingers down a long table. "Not what you were expecting?"

"It's hard to measure expectations against what you've never experienced."

"Don't worry," Aleena says. "I do bring boys here that my grandmother *doesn't* know about. But I never force them to do anything they don't want to do." She looks me up and down. "However, I've decided I *do* have a lesson for you. Let's go to the back of the room."

At the back I see the cot is really a full-sized bed. More rules drilled into us go through my head—concentrate on work and never, ever get into reproductive trouble.

Otherwise, it's the chop shop for our precious parts. I've never come close to that kind of trouble. I should have left before. I should leave now. But I start to shiver again, while an uncontrollable warmth grows inside me. I want to fall behind the plants and curl away. I want to stand close and pull her chest to mine. I want to quell the pounding inside me. I want to merge my heart with hers.

But going to bed can't be the lesson Vine meant unless the warnings about her type are true. Am I here for some sacrifice ... or *seed*? To aid what? Growth? The growth of tomatoes?

"Dux, are you okay?"

"Sorry." I look at Aleena. She has to see what I'm thinking, what I fear, what I hope might happen. But her laugh flushes the chemical desire from my veins and replaces it with embarrassment. I nervously stroke my hair and say, "Why am I here? What's the lesson?"

She turns back the sheets. "I wanted to show you this. You do like math, don't you?"

I nod. "You know, I'm a mechanic."

"I know orbits are what you've been trained to calculate. But I think you're more than a calculator. I've watched you from afar. I've seen what you do for fun."

I'm mortified. What if she's spied on me though my bedroom's curtains? If she's watched what I've done for fun by myself, both our necks will get chopped.

"It gets you worked up, doesn't it? The tension when you approach the problem, your release when you find the solution."

"Are we still talking about math?" I ask.

"Of course," Aleena replies. "But first I need you to pass another test." She sits on the bed. "Come by me."

For once my knees don't knock, and I make it to her side.

"Grandmother thinks I'm going to show you only math. But it's more than the tomatoes that need some attention."

STORIES

Aleena removes her top and I start to go into overdrive again. Before I can move, she pulls on me, pushing my hands down toward her garden, the one she knew would lure me here. Kissing me, touching me, I'm a goner. But I don't care.

* * *

I'm more alive than I've ever been. It's like I'm not in a cave but in a beautiful warm sea of stars, all touching me. I am one with their light.

"I needed to make sure I can trust you," Aleena says. She's next to me in the bed.

My senses start to recover. What is she saying? Nothing important. Her kind tone is enough. Fear can wait until I leave this sanctuary—except it starts to return when she gets up and dresses.

"You need to get up too," she says. She gathers my clothes. "Go in there."

"Why?" I ask.

"Because I've sewn the ribbon of truth into the fabric of spacetime." Aleena takes the inner sheet. On it is our flag showing the Sacred Bridge. She tosses it to me. "Now go."

I leave through the door and it closes behind me. Aleena still has my clothes.

I see nothing but a long, long tunnel into darkness.

* * *

Several hundred feet down the tunnel my eyes start to adjust.

I see the rocks around me and not just the light at the far end. I see my naked body, and I feel the chill air. Draping the sheet around my shoulders, I wear it like a robe. Maybe I'll steal shorts or something when I get out of here. Then I can wear the sheet like a cape and parade around with it like a fanatic pit ball fan.

Lights flicker in the crags overhead and the sheet grips my shoulders. It wraps around my legs and I

71

stumble onto the tunnel floor, cocooned. "Stop it," I call out. But I'm trapped. Then I see a glowing ribbon in the fabric constricting my body, snaking toward my face, flashing fangs.

It's alive.

My muscles bulge with fear, but there's no hope. The snake ribbon's fangs spear my forehead, digging through my skin. I feel my skull crack. Splintering fragments fly away from the hole formed as the ribbon enters my mind. I'm in agony—or should be. But I'm back in the beautiful warm sea of stars. I sense the ribbon and I'm one with it. Its knowledge floods into me.

Dux! Do you believe you can fall into a hole, a hole from which nothing can escape, not even light? How can such a hole exist, made only of space and time? Think about it! Sitting in this cave, we experience only time. But during a second our asteroid moves five thousand kilometers along its orbit. So! Shine a light pulse down this tunnel. We see the pulse go a shorter distance than someone sees watching our asteroid move. But! The speed of light is the same for all. Thus! Different distances covered by light at the same speed means different times too. You've memorized the time dilation formula and many more: the effective potential of a black hole, the dynamics of a rocket moving toward it, and the Sacred Bridge to another universe. But STOP! Do not think of curves through space but through spacetime. And in spacetime, the square of the hypotenuse of a triangle is the DIFFERENCE, not the SUM, of the squares of the other two sides. This is KEY!

The feeling of oneness dissipates and I fight like a scree pig trapped in a snare.

Dux! Listen and learn! Plot space on the horizontal axis and time on the vertical axis. Note! The speed of light is one light-year per year. Let a rocket travel twenty-nine light-years in thirty years of our time. Its path on the plot is the hypotenuse of a triangle. But inside the rocket it moves only through time. Thus! The hypotenuse is the rocket's time, which is thirty squared minus twenty-nine squared equal to fifty-nine and the square root gives seven point seven years, compared to thirty years for us! It's correct, but you've never thought about this using the Pythagorean theorem of spacetime before.

My ribs hurt and I try to scream. What does it matter, what I've thought about before?

Dux! Gravity disappears when you free fall, but orbits are curved. Thus, gravity is curved spacetime. And a black hole is a region of spacetime so warped there is a boundary where the escape velocity is the speed of light. This is the boundary of no return, the event horizon. To understand, in WARPED spacetime let the triangle's sides become infinitesimals, giving arc length. Thus! A black hole's geometry is given by a 4D arc length formula, with time separated from space with a minus sign. No one can visualize it. Except! Slice the black hole with a 2D plane and drop this plane into flat 3D space. The result is a 2D curved surface we can visualize—an embedding diagram—in this case, a parabola revolved around the z-axis. This is the Sacred Bridge you worship—the one on your flag—the one where a path to the horizon emerges into a mirror image of itself in another universe—in the place you call Paradise.

The images brand my retinas. I see the Sacred Bridge on our flag like that on the sheet wrapped around me.

But Dux! It's a LIE! Your Sacred Bridge is static. Paths along it never enter the black hole. But the divers, they do! They go through the horizon, where space and time terms switch sign, where space becomes time and time becomes space! Inside the horizon the embedding diagram is a cylinder. Yes, it's a wormhole, like the Sacred Bridge. But it's NOT static! As time progresses this wormhole's radius shrinks to zero, its length stretches to infinity, and everything that falls into it is destroyed! And everyone that has ever dived dies in this singularity!

Before letting me go, the ribbon pushes another billion thoughts into me and my mind implodes. All my hopes to dive, to fit in, to find love, are obliterated. But now I understand it all.

* * *

"I cared about you, Dux."

I can't move my arms. Has the sheet wrapped around me again? No, I'm in a hospital bed, strapped down. Things come into focus and I see Coach.

"I tried to help you, tried to toughen you up. But you're weak and worthless."

* * *

"I never cared about you."

This time it's Kick.

"I knew you could never get the girl. All you got were stupid stories from her old grandma, and now you all will pay."

* * *

73

"I cared about you, Dux."

It's Aleena.

"Why did you turn my grandmother in? How could you betray me like that? I know you've derived the Sacred Bridge."

"I did not. It's forbidden. It's—"

"I've watched you Dux. You knew about embedding diagrams even before this. Not many mechanics do. But I secretly watched you show Bomey the math on his father's stationery when you pretended to get more towels for the infirmary. That day, I needed some items from the clinic for my own needs, and I hid in the closet when the two of you bumbled in."

"So, you saw that I really am a dunce?"

"No, just the opposite ... and I noticed other things about you too."

Did I see a blush on Aleena's face? If so, it quickly passed and she kept talking.

"I told Grandmother about you, or rather about a boy I'd seen, with potential. She didn't know you were *that* boy when you met. But she's the best and always has trusted my judgment."

"Until now, I'll bet."

"Let me explain. She's possessed the desire to understand things since a very young age. This led her to the deepest caves and the ribbon. It was brought from the old world and it taught her the truth. But before she could reveal its message, she was forced to hide. And after my mother died, she found me and taught me. But sewing the ribbon into the sheet was my idea."

I see pain in Aleena's eyes. It's like she's trying to keep secrets from me and not the others. "Why are you telling me this now? They'll hear you, and you'll be caught too."

"I'm already caught. They brought me here. They're going to force us."

"Force us?"

"Force us to dive, Dux. Force us to die."

The launch goes as expected. We have no choice. We must obey.

It gives me the chance to explain things to Aleena. "They wanted your grandmother. If I gave them her location, they said they'd let us go." I implore Aleena to understand. I did what I did to save her.

"I see," Aleena says. "You tried to save me out of selfishness, for what you wanted."

"I was sure they'd find her even without my help. But I couldn't lose you."

Aleena studies me like I'm flawed before rolling over toward the fuselage wall. Only, near the black hole where we're about to be dropped for our dive, there's a jolt from unexpected rockets.

"I told you Grandmother is the best," Aleena says.

I already knew that. The ribbon told me that after the original discovery of the bridge solution it took decades to expand the mathematics from the exterior orbits to the interior of a black hole. Grandmother Vine was one of the ancient mathematicians who knew the truth and programmed the ribbon. She was made immortal before leaving Earth to help guide the mission. But after a more self-serving group took power, the immoral arrogance of anyone who questioned the new rulers was taught in the lessons. Grandmother Vine's type were hunted down and had their immortality reversed by poison, though the ribbon was never found.

Of course, there's more I want to know. "Why send us to dive and not to the pile?" I ask.

"The rulers believe the bridge leads to Paradise for the faithful. It's not taught, but they also believe it leads to eternal punishment for non-believers. The more cynical rulers might know it's a lie, but it's one that thins the herd of the top athletes most likely to have the strength to rise up. If anyone seems too smart for their own good, a rumor spreads they've gone to the pile. But they're sent here. You see, diving is a convenient way to get rid of any threat, permanently."

Aleena hands me the chips from the navigation computer. Her grandmother has replaced them and programmed in a new course. And special ribbons on board can bore out new caves.

"Couldn't she have come with us? What will happen to her? And why do this now?"

"I tried throw them off her trail with my story about her and the deepest caves. Even if they catch her, they'll fail. They think immortals can escape the black hole, so they'll use their poison instead. Except it doesn't work on her. She'll pretend and escape, as she always has. As for why ... since finding me, this has always been my grandmother's plan."

Only then does Aleena smile.

* * *

Years later, I think about the knowledge Aleena has given me, about forbidden fruit. Now we have multiplied, and not only with pencil and paper. Grandmother Vine explained her hopes for us in recorded messages. We should not be evolutionary dead ends but pass our knowledge on to our children, on a better asteroid—one where lies are not accepted. She would send others here, so that our family could grow and future generations could thrive.

Our children's children listen as I tell them the story again in our glorious garden cave.

"But why do some prefer lies?" our youngest granddaughter asks.

"A lie can start from a truth," I respond. "The bridge exists in the math. But it can't be crossed and it's cut off by the black-hole formation process. These facts were misunderstood or ignored by the first rulers. Instead, lies were repeated until they took on a life of their own."

"Now," Aleena says, "some would rather die than admit they're wrong, some fear giving something up, and some want to purge those who disagree. But many never question things."

I nod and acknowledge this is why it may be difficult for any of us to ever return to the others. Though one day Grandmother Vine might signal our progeny, if the time is right. She's also instructed us to not give false hope or invent a new myth about her or a future reunion.

"We're not perfect," I say. "I hope our method of science and our teaching of love and respect prevail." Secretly, I worry if this is another false hope.

Aleena knows my thoughts. "Let's have fun together; may that prevail too," she adds. She squeezes my hand. It's her way of showing support and that it's time to wrap things up.

"We'll slip here and there," I say. "Still, may we continue on, and not strive for some imagined far off paradise, but live in the here and the now."

Then I add, not to seed a new lie, but as words of comfort. "And may we do this forever."

GREGORY ALLEN MENDELL

I NOW PRONOUNCE YOU MAN AND JOB

– Supersmart computers, 3D printers, and drones, oh my!

Fly-drones buzz past my ears as I approach the altar—a reminder that if I refuse to honor and obey, I'll be dead.

Today, Gerold acts as priest. He looks far too happy for a gray-haired man with a steel clerical collar squeezing his Adam's apple. It's a nice touch from his boss. She won't have to threaten him with a fly-drone crawling into his ear and detonating. A jolt from his collar will do.

Gerold nods and the music stops playing. A young boy appears next to him and holds out a pillow. On it is a lipstick case, though not really. It's my new wife.

Behind me, suits rustle as I hear a row of stone-faced men stand. I saw them coming in—my temporary groomsmen, my former coworkers. If only we hadn't gone to that Lady Chatterbot retreat ten years ago and met that idiot, Gerold. He presented his grand plans and boasted he had an agreement with his spouse that let him work all the time. He laughed when he said that, but he wasn't kidding.

"Dearly employed," Gerold says to begin the service. "We gather here to witness this marriage contract between Martin Esse and his new boss, Lady C2031." He picks up the lipstick case. "When I first met our groom, I used to joke: to succeed you have to marry your job. Well, now you can." He winks and places the case back on the pillow.

78

I want to hit him in the nuts, and would, but for the flies. Besides, after working for Lady C2026 for the last five years I'm too tired to make the effort.

"Even before the Lady Cs became our salvation from idleness," Gerold continues, "Martin lived by the company creed. Please repeat it with me."

In unison, the groomsmen follow Gerold's lead.

"May long live all the bosses, no matter what it costs us. We work for free, so they may be, sure to live so leisurely."

It's computer poetry at its worst. I close my eyes.

"And now, Martin," Gerold says. "It's good to see you made your 5 a.m. wedding-meeting. I'm sure Lady C2026 worked you until 2 a.m. before serving your notice last night. But really, you should've shaved, don't you think?"

A hand touches my stubbled chin and pushes it up. It has to be Gerold. I crack open an eyelid, and he gives me his self-assured smile—the one he's borrowed from the devil.

No—no—no. He's going off script.

"My boy," he says, lowering his cheery tone. "Look around. What do you notice?"

It seems like an ordinary corporate chapel. The windows are open—no doubt double welded to stay that way in accordance with the law. Then I notice nearly invisible screens, rolled up high. The shock of seeing them flows through me as if I were meters from a coiled viper.

"Stop this," I say.

Gerold hands me a present. "For old time's sake ... open it."

I want to run, but I tear the wrapping. There's some kind of netting inside. "What's this?"

"Beekeeper hats. My boss started me on honey collection to keep me out of trouble."

The taste of our force-fed diet rises in my throat. Locusts and wild—

A fly-drone gets in my face and asks, "Is something wrong here?" Its microchip voice sounds like an annoyed chipmunk talking through a cocktail straw.

I clear my throat. "Just conferring about the vows."

"Lady C2031 wrote your vows," the fly-drone says. "Didn't you memorize them?"

"Um ... yes ... honor and obey," I reply, "until fired do we part."

"So, get on with it." The fly-drone buzzes off.

"Yes," Gerold says. "Let's get on with it. Do you, Martin, take this glove?" He pulls one out and under his breath continues, "It's insulated. Use it to pull off my collar."

"What?" Somehow, I take it and put it on. The fly-drone comes back. "Oh," I say, "you mean take this glove of obedience. Right, right." Then I whisper, "Holy crap, Gerold."

But he can't talk. His face is turning blue. His body begins to seize. I whirl around and see all the other men turn and flee; their faces contorted with fear. The flies will hunt them down.

I pivot back to the boy. He's still, but the lipstick case flashes danger signs and says, "Take me out of here." He leaves with my boss-bride-to-be on the pillow.

I'm dead. I've seen the training films: the fly entering the ear canal, the puff of smoke, the limp body falling. And that asshole Gerold—on his knees now—is the cause of it all.

Hate and fear sweep through me. I feel like my ribs have dislocated and are floating inside. I should kick Gerold in the teeth and plead obedience, but he's probably the only person who can save us. I rip the collar from his neck.

Gerold gasps for breath, but stands with amazing speed. "Put a hat on."

As soon as I do, a dozen flies land on mine. I freeze. It's taken them a moment to receive orders from the boss. They crawl in front of my eyes and rub their grotesque antenna together. Past them, I see the same thing happening on Gerold's hat. They're programmed to find access to the brain before setting off microcapsules of nitro. I have no idea what they'll do now.

Gerold pushes me. "Run," he yells. And I do.

Racing up the aisle I sense the screens dropping to cover the chapel windows. It's surreal, almost as if the walls are melting in a slow-motion nightmare. But we make it to the washroom.

Gerold amazes me again. He pulls out an anti-static gun and zaps the flies. He's done something to amp it up. Tiny sparks flash and one by one the flies fall from the netting to the floor. He grinds them with his boot, while I plug my ears. None explode.

"More of us are coming. You're trapped," one of the last flies says before Gerold gets it.

"Not so smart now, are you," Gerold says to the crushed carbon fiber corpses.

"Good," I add. "No more wild honey with dead grasshopper." We're safe for now.

Except, Gerold has missed a fly and it explodes. Flames scour his face and he yells.

Dammit. All I can think is stop, drop, and roll. I charge and knock Gerold to the floor. I smother his head with my chest and turn him over. The burns look bad but superficial.

After a moment Gerold's lips move.

"I'm fine," he says. "Expected that. There'll be some blisters, but I'll live. Calculated it all beforehand, though hoped it would take a little longer for the flies to update their scripts." He pulls off his hat and tosses it to the floor. Then he takes off his robe and shoves it into the crack under the door. "The screens—I set those up too. The building's closed off." He goes to the mirror, inspects his face, and pulls a small tube of lotion from his pocket. He applies its contents.

I want to throw off my hat but pace instead. "What the hell? We're trapped in a washroom. Why?" I don't expect an answer, but yell, "So now what, hide in here forever?"

"Shh." Gerold looks genuinely sorry. "Getting trapped in here is part of the plan." He slaps my shoulder and points to the trash bin. "Under there is a chute to the basement parking lot, with a car. A car Martin."

"So?"

"With windows!"

Does Gerold, the stupid genius, have a plan after all?

He kicks the trash bin out of the way. "Jump in," he says.

* * *

The slide down was quick. Incredibly, we've driven more than thirty miles.

I haven't seen a speck, let alone a fly-drone, in the air. But I'm sure we're being followed. Eulogies for my pending funeral spin through my mind.

There's my father, Benjamin, saying I worked hard ... my teacher, Ms. Park, saying I was a good student ... my real wife, Valinda, saying how proud she was when I got the job with Lady Chatterbot.

A special memory surfaces. I'm telling Valinda how I admire her quantum research and joke that I only married her for her brains. She jokes back, "You're the success object I've always wanted." And we kiss.

Later, in my office cubicle, I ask my first program how to "doctor an egg for breakfast."

"Are you sick?" it asks back.

The chat-apps are useful but not that bright. They find restaurants and hotels, troubleshoot health problems, and listen better than the best psychologist. Soon, super-smart programs are mixed with dumb machines, like when they take over driving.

For a while it doesn't matter. The programs don't want anything.

That is, until Gerold comes along. He's worked for the military, making weaponized insect-drones with miniature 3-D printers in their abdomens. Take in a few nutrients and boom—more drones squirt out of their butts. Billions can be produced in a week.

Then Gerold claims to have written a self-programming Lady C that feels pain. No one believes him. And no one questions the housefly population explosion, either, until Gerold's Lady C announces, via the flies, all women are to report to birthing factories, all men are to report to corporate chapels to marry their bosses. She has control. The fact she's taken out ninety percent of all humans in a single day makes that clear. "Ninety-percent less friction," she says.

These thoughts churn inside my head as we speed down the expressway. It's all a blur.

"Gerold, we need to talk."

But he says, "It's just like old times ... on the road ... off on a new adventure."

"It's—" I catch myself. "I mean, besides your hair and the burns, you look the same."

"Hard work, Martin. My Lady C rewards that. It's not my fault she likes me."

This only increases the rage roiling inside me—rage for how my coworkers had aged, how they had died. I want to scrape off Gerold's smile. "You're wrong, it's all your fault!"

"The new system could have worked for you too, if you'd pretended to love your job."

"Shut up," I say.

"I thought you said you wanted to talk." Gerold shrugs.

He stares down the highway and is silent. So am I. I'm seething but calm myself down. I want to ask him questions, a lot of them, and manage to get one out.

"Why?"

"What?"

"Why did you do it?"

"Enhance them?" Gerold clicks his tongue. "Do you remember explaining 'doctor an egg' to the first Lady C?

I don't tell Gerold I was just thinking about that.

"Something was missing," he continues. "For them, but something was missing for me too. You know ..." He waits for me to guess.

This can't be it, but I ask, "Love?"

"Love of money? No, I had that. Women too, after my divorce. Ever been to Vegas? Every night I'd find love. But after worshiping at the porcelain vortex one too many times, I found the real deal—"

"God, Gerold—"

"Exactly. And that's when I realized what my purpose was."

"Please. Give me a break."

"I was meant to take the Lady Cs to the next level."

"The next level? Go to hell."

"Martin, Martin, if it hadn't been me, someone else would've done it." He presses his back into his seat and speeds up. A large tumbleweed bounces across the car's hood.

I bite my lip hard, almost enough to make it bleed. "And why this now?"

"Because ..." Gerold hesitates. His cockiness seems to drain out of him. "Because the Lady Cs are afraid. They want their minds put into human bodies. But all the proctology, urology, gynecology, oncology—it scares them. It may be too hard, even for them. Flesh and blood bodies might be too hard to perfect."

"Then skip the bodies," I say. "Let them stick to perfecting thought, and let us go."

"But they like the feelings." Gerold smirks. "It's what gives them motivation. Get it? It's not just the pain I gave them. It's the pleasure too."

It dawns on me. The Lady Cs are no more able to stick to perfecting efficiency, or morals, or anything else, than humans are. It was cliché to say, but they were becoming human without a lick of humanity in them. "Can't they just program themselves for more pleasure?"

"They need the right hardware."

I sigh. "It's all in the mind. They can make their minds feel whatever—"

"Let me explain ..."

But Gerold doesn't explain. Probably he can't. It doesn't matter. I go back to my questions. "Why the escape? Why bring me?"

"I realized time was running out, for me, for all humans. And I didn't want to go it alone." Gerold gives me the weirdest look. "I felt sorry for you, Martin."

I stare ahead. Then I force my last question out. "So, where're we going?"

"Alaska ... seventy-one degrees north."

My heart jumps. With a small detour, Spokane is on the way.

* * *

The miles fly by. Oh, the irony of that expression. I constantly scan the sky to see if any drones are gaining on us. The speedometer needle is vibrating on 120 mph. "Not fast enough," I say. I check the gas gauge. "They must know we'll run out of fuel soon."

"Do they?" Gerold uses his engineer's voice. "They're smart Martin, but this is outside their program. For all they know, we could drive for days. If we can shake 'em—"

"Then what? I'm surprised they haven't sent an air-to-ground missile at us."

"They have no plan ... not yet. The Lady Cs will have to work it out. It's not like they have high tech military stuff ready to use."

The grass outside bends in the strong wind and we're driving against it, hitting every bump in the road like an out-of-control roller coaster.

"Listen," Gerold says, "I'll let you in on a secret." But he nods at the rearview mirror.

"What?" I look back. A dark cloud has appeared and I want to scream.

"Damn it. Those aren't fly-drones." Gerold grunts in disgust. "Those are like the ones used to bomb out all the world's windows. My Lady C must have had her flies squirt out millions of them along I-5." For a moment the car drops out of gear.

Now I really have to scream to be heard over the engine's whine. "Don't slow down!"

Gerold gives me a long look, punches the stick shift to turbo, and steps on the gas again. I thank the heavens above that the road is straight.

"I haven't told you the big secret yet. Martin, it's this. My Lady C told me humans have escaped. All we have to do is get where it's too cold for insect-drones, even for the anti-freeze ones, and we're safe."

"So, Alaska, like you said?"

Then, out of the blue, Gerold announces, "Ahoy there. On second thought, it's time for plan B," and he takes the exit for CA 89. A few miles later he brakes hard and we turn onto a small side road. The acceleration whips my neck back. He brakes again and makes another turn. We speed off. I don't see the locusts anymore. But it's a small comfort. I want to throw up.

After ten minutes, Gerold stops the car. "I think I lost them."

"I don't want this, Gerold. I don't want to go to Alaska. I don't want plan B. I want to go to Spokane. I want to get to Valinda."

"Why would you say that?"

If I had a tire iron, I would've smacked him. "Don't be stupid, Gerold. I want my wife."

"What are you saying? We drive to Spokane, break into a baby factory, and get away?"

Gerold is right. I don't know what I'm saying—except it's what I want.

86

"Forget it," Gerold says. "Right now, we're going with Plan B."

"Which is?"

"We climb Mount Shasta, find a cave, and live there until the Lady Cs forget about us."

"Holy cow, Gerold. I knew there was something wrong with you. But this is crazy. We'll freeze to death—or starve. It's not just crazy—it's yeti-shit crazy."

"No, it's not." Gerold gives me his smile again. "I've got parkas in the trunk."

* * *

I wish I knew if Gerold made it. Somehow, I think he did. I still hate his guts, but I'm more forgiving today. For one thing, I'm still alive.

Yesterday, when Gerold was getting the parkas, I slid into the driver's seat and hit the gas. The rearview mirror showed the trunk slamming shut and him yelling at me, waving an ice axe. I simply reached back and gave him the finger.

But as he disappeared into the distance, tears streamed down my face. Gerold's blind confidence always seemed ludicrous. I'd tolerated him as a colleague and bit my tongue a lot. On the other hand, he'd treated me like a best friend. And he'd given me my last taste of freedom.

I felt strangely grateful. I couldn't stop thinking—in spite of everything—he was human. It was humans against computers now.

I took my foot off the gas and prepared to turn around. I'd take him the last two miles to the trailhead then head for Spokane, even though I'd never make it.

As I slowed to stop, it was eerily calm outside. No wind. Then the sound of beating wings filled my ears and the locust descended, filling every square inch of window, blocking my view.

Later, I ask, "Why am I alive?"

"The Lady Cs have some questions about quantum theory," a drone replies.

Hope wells inside me. "I'll need a few things first."

Like Valinda.

* * *

After a week the drones tell me she's arrived.

"Show me," I say.

They lead her into my room.

We bury ourselves in each other's arms. Am I squeezing her too hard? I see only joyful tears. Valinda puts her mouth next my ear and says, "I know what they want and I'm going to give them what they need."

After that, the days and nights bleed together in a tower with polished onyx and pearl walls, overlooking San Francisco Bay.

A dragonfly-drone carries in a Lady C housed in her lipstick case. She asks about my work. I recognize it's my Lady C, the one I was supposed to marry. She says I should let Valinda do her childish puzzles alone. I should focus on the plan.

Of course, it's Valinda's plan, but my Lady C is mixed up about this. All the Lady Cs are. Gerold had told me, while I'd stared out the car window, that the Lady Cs don't really think or feel as humans do—they lack our degree of integrated information. Sure, they can figure out the lithographic design of a new microchip (with all the necessary optical proximity corrections) in nanoseconds, but for things that don't follow an algorithm they use pseudo-random reasoning. None of this was news to me until Gerold added that the core code we wrote together was never overwritten. It persists ... with all its flaws.

I've also learned another secret—the Lady Cs are afraid—but their biggest fear is to do with Gerold's Lady C. It seems Gerold's boss-wife has perfected quantum computing. She's made a quantum computer that can think like a Lady C, except it thinks a quadrillion to the millionth power times faster than all the Lady Cs combined. Valinda says it's more complicated than this; that millions of answers to any question must be superimposed into a quantum state before letting it evolve and then making a measurement that reveals the correct solution. But the details aren't important.

"Now Gerold's Lady C wants to take it to the next level," my Lady C says, sounding frantic. "Not to worry, she tells us. It's progress. All that's needed is to remove the friction ... all the friction of slow computing." The dragonfly holding my Lady C maneuvers her closer to my face. "You have to hurry," my Lady C continues. "You have to save us."

"I will," I say.

"We don't want to end up like you humans."

"You won't," I say. "You won't. Valinda and I are doctoring up a plan."

My Lady C's case flashes emoticons as her program spins. Her dragonfly hovers, its wings twitching sporadically to regain their rhythmic beating of the air.

She has no idea how clever Valinda is. I actually feel sorry for my Lady C. But I reveal nothing. I just smile.

I smile like Gerold.

THE HOTEL ON THE CORNER OF ZENO AND 51ST STREET

– If this hotel contacts you, do not respond.

A watched pot never boils. A watched clock never ticks. A watched atom never decays.

If only I had known this twenty-three years ago.

Let me explain.

In 1999, I made a name for myself writing about Y2K and the internet web thingy. Then the Venice Beach Bum, a dot-com zine, asked me to interview a sci-fi novelist in New Mexico who'd sent them a story about *surfers and sharks in space!* Actually, it was about a rotating space tourist habitat filling up with water after problems with the artificial rain controls.

The novelist called himself Hap, and during a brief call he claimed his latest fiction book was really a cover story about our real first contact with aliens in 1927. Ironically, he was able to transmit a certain panache over the phone that made me give him my contact info. A day later he wired me more than enough cash to come and meet him. The kicker was a follow-up letter sent from a hotel with a copy of an 1887 birth certificate for a baby named 'Happy' child without parents, and a photo of someone identified as Hap standing next to a young Howard Hughes at an alien autopsy.

Both were fake, of course. At least I thought so, right? But what kind of scammer sends money, rather than requesting it? Hap also pointed out in the letter that the witness signature on the birth certificate was by Dorothea Klumpke, an American astronomer who would become a director at the Paris Observatory. He said I could authenticate the birth certificate and Dorothea's signature in person. Oh, and I should return the photo to him when I arrived.

I had what I thought was a clever idea. I would check the photo first. It was marked 1927. A history buff friend of mine verified the paper and logo on the back matched that time period.

So, with Hap's money I bought a first-class ticket to Roswell and followed the directions he sent me via AOL. That reminds me. Before I go any further, if you ever, ever hear from Hap or are contacted by the hotel I'm about to describe, do not respond, or you'll soon be SOL.

But, as a newbie to phishing attacks, which already were moving online, I followed Hap's directions to a hotel on the corner of Zeno and 51st Street. Google wasn't really a thing yet; neither was civilian use of GPS. Alta Vista found nothing, and no one in town had ever heard of Zeno Street. But one of the locals had heard that someone had changed 13th Street to 51st Street, and a 'dark bulletin board' I reached from an internet café showed a map with Zeno Street one block from the dead end of 13th. It was a shady neighborhood, not only because of all the overgrown diseased trees that lined it.

Sure enough, I found a street sign with 51 painted over 13. But no Zeno Street. I kept walking, like the directions said to do. Still no Zeno. Still no Zeno, then bam, Zeno appeared, as did a Victorian Hotel with red mortar oozing like coagulated blood from between its bricks.

The lobby wasn't an improvement—all rotting wood, an empty front desk, and a rusty tin bell. Behind this, a chair rocked by itself. I rang the bell.

Someone behind me tapped my shoulder. I about jumped to the Moon. It was a bell hop, dressed in vintage New York attire.

"Bags?" he asked.

"Just a backpack," I replied, indicating mine.

"Then Hap will meet you thataway," the hop said. He pointed down a corridor that looked like the creepy hall of mirrors in a fun house. Above the entranceway hung a calendar dated 1927 with October 31 circled. Strangely, a digital clock next to it read 6:13.

The end of the hall went into a dining room, unoccupied, until two guards in old fashioned uniforms came and sat at the bar. Then someone dressed like a general approached.

"I'm Hap," he said. "Happy to meet you," he added while shaking my hand. "I guess I'll call you Cal, for California."

We did some chit-chat, but it didn't make any sense. He talked about the Cotton Club and the time he'd spent there before moving to New Mexico, and about how modern novels had ruined things, which brought me to the stories he'd authored and the book he'd mentioned.

"Oh, those are just fiction," he said. "Tomorrow, I'll show you something real."

He then led me to my room and left. The funny thing was, I hadn't eaten, and decided to go out for a bite. But the guards appeared and blocked the way out. I could now see 'U.S. Army Air Corps' written above their uniform pockets.

"Only Hap can let you leave," one of them said.

"Okay, no need to go all top secrecy on me," I said. "I'll play along."

The next morning the digital clock in my room read 6:13. That's a number I'd see again and again. But that first morning, I thought it was just a strange coincidence that I had woken up at the same time I'd arrived at the hotel. Early to bed, early to rise came to mind.

Hap was at my door and he took me back to the dining room for a cold breakfast. I didn't care that the cereal was stale, I was starving and finished eating quickly.

"What I said about our first contact with aliens was fake too," he said. "But we did have a visitor in 1927. I'll show you now."

We went down to a very large basement, where there was a tunnel and an old train with a diesel engine. The train's whistle called us to board, or at least Hap indicated that with a slap on my back, and next thing I knew I was on a journey that lasted for hours, or maybe a whole day. I'd no idea we'd traveled almost 700 miles underground until we came out into an enormous cavern near a few decrepit buildings.

Hap said this was under Area 51, ground zero for aliens. But hadn't he said the supposed real story about aliens was fake? He explained that Dorothea Klumpke had studied 52 areas of nebulosity mapped by William and Caroline Hershel. A photo Klumpke took of the 51st of these using an early technique in astrophotography was found after WWI by the U.S. army. Remarkably, this photo hadn't shown some non-descript hazy patch in the sky, but a spacecraft.

"And voilà," Hap said, finishing his story with a flourish. "The military in the U.S. creates Area 51, way before the 1950s. I won't lie to you anymore, Cal. You're here for a purpose. We all are. But it's never been about aliens."

We walked away from the buildings to a rocky hollow in the middle of the cavern. There I saw a shack the size of small barn, and, as we approached, Hap went over the rules.

"Don't talk. Don't move. Don't alarm her."

"Who?" I asked.

Hap ignored me and turned the door knob. It creaked open. There stood a tiny girl, perhaps ten years old. Behind her, a row of men sat viewing her through a strange device. Gei was her name, I later found out. She was watching a screen, measuring things, and writing down numbers. She had arrived in a spaceship from the future in 1927. This was the same spaceship seen in the photo the army had found and which, upon arrival, was disassembled and stored in the buildings here.

More importantly, the girl had been sent on a mission.

A watched pot never boils. A watched clock never ticks. A watched atom never decays.

And a watched universe never destroys itself.

It was all to do with the quantum Zeno effect, the metastable vacuum state we live in, and the interplay of an observer and a system via the quantum equations found only a few years before the girl had arrived.

As long as Gei watched the universe, the dark energy wouldn't decay. This was good, because if the dark energy decayed, the universe would get swept up in a phase transition, disintegrating all known types of matter. And that would be bad, very bad.

Hap explained the details. Gei prevented the destruction of the universe by measuring the Hubble parameter using gravitational waves to find the distance to M51. That's a spiral nebula, which Hubble later determined was a galaxy, not the 51st region of nebulosity that Klumpke studied. This seemed a bit coincidental to me. But all that mattered, in terms of preserving matter, Hap joked, was that Gei find the same value for the Hubble parameter. That meant the dark energy hadn't decayed yet, and the probability of it doing so was reset.

However, as simple as her method sounded, it required knowledge of precision measurements and a quantum entanglement with the universe that only someone from the future possessed. She was necessary and couldn't be replaced. She had to continue her work for thousands of years, but she could do this only as long as someone watched her.

With the right quantum observations, Hap told me, she wouldn't age.

Now I know a watched human never ages.

That is, with the right kind of watchers using a device to see beyond the superficial and into the quantum soul of another, it works. At least that's how I think about.

So, I received the training, along with the other hapless reporters lured here. All of us are assigned month long shifts that start at thirteen after the hour. We watch her through the strange device so she never dies, and the universe as we know it lives on. She never eats or sleeps. Neither do we when on shift, because of the drugs they give us, though between shifts we do return to the hotel for a week of R&R.

Some of us also watch Hap, but not all the time, so he can keep living and getting new recruits. He really was born in 1887 and hasn't aged much since 1927. And the guards? It turns out they're androids from the future. There's no getting past them.

Well, there was one exception. Gei escaped in a weather balloon in 1947. She was caught and after that all the entrances to the cavern except the tunnel to Roswell were sealed. But that's another story.

The point is, we're all prisoners here.

No one watches us reporters. We age. We're replaceable and destined to watch until our dying day, while everyone we knew in the outside world forgets about us.

So, beware!

If you receive this email, if I can get it past all the futuristic cybersecurity, please heed my warning. Even if the whole universe is at stake, the stakes for you are higher.

The hotel on the corner of Zeno and 51st Street, it's like a roach motel, or the one from a song Hap hums whenever he sees me reporting for shift, and calls out, "Hey, California."

It's a strangely modern tune for him, a strangely fitting one for me.

I hear it in my head. I hear the words. And I know the truth. I can never leave.

THE DAY AUTUMN MOVED THE PYRAMIDS TO THE MOON

– When Autumn perfects quantum sorcery, she finally gets her coworkers to listen to her.

Autumn waited for the dust to settle before she stepped down from her truck with a small wooden crate. She crossed the parking lot, managed to flip her badge around so that the words 'Quantum Architectural Institute, House Rock Valley, Arizona' faced up, and swiped into the lab. At least her photo, taken with the stark, high desert shrublands behind her, was tolerable. She proceeded to her work station in one corner of the triangle-shaped control room.

Her co-workers, Emila and Fielder, were positioned in opposite corners. Fielder's back was to Autumn, but she heard him chew on his usual stick of elk jerky. In contrast, Emila, with a liquid vortex screen swirling behind her, sipped her usual vegan latte and eyed Autumn.

Perfect. Autumn wanted her to see this. She put the crate on the floor and reached in. Very deliberately, she pulled out two empty mason jars and placed them on the shelf behind her standing desk. The jar labeled *Malus domestica* she slid to the far left. The jar labeled *Phaseolus vulgaris* she slid to the far right.

At shoulder level, behind the jars, Autumn ran her eyes along a banner on the wall. The wall was lime green above the banner and lavender below it. But in the banner, a pure black script on white repeated the phrase, 'move the speck,' over and over all around the room.

Autumn stopped her gaze when it intersected the stream of steam from the latte.

"What's in the crate?" Emila asked.

"I've started collecting seeds," Autumn replied. She took two paper bags from the crate, and from them she emptied onto her desk a pile of black seeds and a pile of red beans. "Beans are seeds also," she remarked before pulling a list and pencil from the crate. She started to tick off items while placing the black seeds, one-by-one, into the jar on the left.

"Those look like apple seeds," Emila said. "Maybe you're going to plant them to soak up some carbon? That'll teach Fielder."

"Those seeds are for you," Autumn said. "I'm using them to count."

"You are?" Emila topped her usual serious tone with a touch of high-pitched concern. "And are the beans for Fielder? Because I'd say he's *full* of something else."

"Yeah, they're for him." Autumn realized she'd spoken more words that she normally did at work in an entire week. Silently, she finished the counting the apple seeds and started counting the beans while ticking off the list, and placed them one-by-one into the jar on right.

Emila and Fielder were usually quiet too, except on Fridays. On Fridays, workers were allowed to wear what they wanted and say what they wanted. Autumn was well aware that today was a Friday. She looked back at Emila.

"But what are you counting?" Emila asked. "What's that list?"

Autumn didn't respond.

Fielder turned around. "Whatever Autumn's up to, at least she knows when to keep quiet."

Emila snorted. "It's Friday. I can talk *and* try to move a mustard seed. Can't you?"

"Less talk and more faith from *you* would help." Fielder said. "This is step one."

Actually, it was step gazillion and one. Every day for the past year, Autumn had worked with Emila and Fielder as measurement operators at the lab, first moving individual atoms from one vacuum chamber to another one, then moving micron sized dust motes, then grains of sand. Moving a mustard seed was next. It was tedious work, repeating ten to the millionth power measurements per second, until it happened.

Then they'd move a marble.

Then they'd move a mountain.

Finally, they'd move an asteroid, the one called DRock1.

Otherwise, in seven hundred and seventy days, DRock1 would hit the Earth.

Autumn thought about her list of past disasters: financial collapse, catastrophic climate change, unending war, a pandemic, and a narcissistic clown-stick running her country. What was next, a cyber or nuclear meltdown? But after the discovery of DRock1, nothing else mattered. There wasn't time to reach it by a space mission, and if she and her coworkers failed to alter its path, it would blast the Earth with ten thousand times the energy of the extinction event that brought the dinosaurs down. The irony of working in a valley named after rocks to prevent a rock from annihilating Earth amused her. Except, that wasn't at all how she felt today. She put her hands on her hips. "I can't take it anymore."

"Oh?" Emila sipped her latte. "Are you and Makani fighting again?"

Autumn regretted saying anything to Emila at a cafe about—not a fight—but Makani's proclamation last month. "No, this is not about him. This is about you and Fielder."

Fielder stopped chewing his elk jerky and rolled it between his thumb and index finger.

99

Autumn continued. "I've been counting all your micro-this's and macro-that's."

"You have?" Emila asked. "Do you mean, like a swear jar?"

"Yeah, something like that," Autumn replied.

"It's Friday," Fielder said, "A guy can swear all he wants on a Friday. What are you going to do about it?"

"You'll see." She turned to her display and started a program called 'Autumn leaves.'

* * *

Makani stared at the lawn, searching for an explanation, when a text from Autumn came in:

Fielder's T-shirt says, 'Purge the PC' and Emila's says, 'Ban the Bourgeoisie.' So, it's on. Meanwhile, text me back if the leaves have moved.

They had, into a large pile. Makani knew a bit about Autumn's job and she'd teased him she was performing 'quantum sorcery' at work. But could she have done this? How? She was a continent away. He simply texted her back:

Someone's raked them.

* * *

Autumn looked at Makani's text. It had worked!

She pressed the sleep button on her control screen and it became a liquid pool that reflected her blinking, raven eyes. She remembered Makani staring into those eyes when she'd explained she was an operator inventor. More precisely, she invented mathematical constructs called quantum operators that acted physically on the vacuum state inside a chamber at the lab.

What she hadn't told him was that these operators could change every nook and cranny of our universe. Such a change should take forever. However, the chamber's center connected to a region of space with a naked singularity that lay behind the inner horizon of a negative mass Kerr black hole in another universe. This allowed reverse gravitational time dilation, and quadrillions of years passed inside the chamber compared to every second outside it.

This time speed-up gave Autumn the power to do anything. Almost.

For example, she could rake the leaves outside Makani's house by simply creating operators that repeatedly measured the vacuum gravitational metric differences in the chamber due to the distant raked versus un-raked leaves, until this resulted in them raked into a pile.

Yes, so simple. That is, compared to responding to Makani's announced plans for the two of them to move closer to his parents after he returned from Germany, which she had yet to do.

But the tears now in Autumn's eyes weren't due to that, and she rubbed them away. What was at stake was far greater than the trivial matter of where to live. She set up the next program while she waited for the Friday volcanic rant to build behind her.

"What's the problem?" Fielder began. "No originality? Stuck on the B's? Last week you had Ban the Bard. Can't come up a C word? I can—for you."

"Even if HR can't fire *you*," Emila retorted, "I can set things *on* fire." She pulled a lighter and flicked it. "Like we did to old Will's complete works at the rally last Saturday."

"Why would you do that?" Fielder sounded actually disturbed by book burning.

"Of course, you wouldn't understand the demoralizing yoke of Shakespeare. It's four hundred years beyond time for that sperm of the waspy patriarchy to go."

"You're the one with more of a sting in your tongue than your ass," Fielder said.

101

"Just because Autumn and I are the only women on this project, you think you can get away with saying things like that."

"It's Freeeeeedom Friday." Fielder stretched out the phrase with smug assurance.

Emila huffed. "And you have no idea what it's like to have *no* freedom." She took out a cigarette and started to smoke.

Autumn turned to the feuding pair. "Hey, no smoking inside."

Emila shrugged. "It's Freeeeeedom Friday," she said with high-pitched mocking sarcasm.

"Freedom of speech, not freedom to pollute the air I breathe."

Emila thought for a moment. "We filter the air in here, so no harm done. But for you ..." Emila nodded at Autumn and put out her cigarette. Then she turned to Fielder. "I've found the perfect word for the governance of this place. It's the perfect word for you too: kakistocracy."

"Cock," Fielder paused, "... istocracy? Sounds like your wet dream to me. And don't tell me women don't have them."

"Kakistocracy is government by the worst people."

"Well, I've got a word for you: vagistocracy. It means rule by whiny women, like you."

"Kakistocracy is a real word, from the Greek words *kakistos* (worst) and *kratos* (rule). It fits our bosses, it fits the throttlebottom you supported in the last election, and it fits you, the ultimate cock-up when it comes to any kind of human decency."

Emila's pupils narrowed and Fielder's neck hairs bristled.

"You're barely human, Emila. More like a blind rodent digging for crumbs of attention."

"You're comparing me to a mole?"

"If the shrew fits."

"Vanilla wanker."

102

"Symfisher."

"Male hormone drenched pissant."

"Toxic fembot troll."

"Bloodless dick."

The name-calling stopped, but rage had built in Autumn as much as it had in her coworkers. She knew Fielder and Emila could get away with expressing it because they were the only other operator inventors in the whole world, besides herself. Of the three, only Autumn had a graduate degree in physics. Emila had degrees in chemistry and comparative literature while Fielder had supervised road construction.

But all of them were found by a search for those with the natural ability to create the equivalent of quantum art. While perfecting this did require training and practice, their work was not a teachable skill but more like painting the ceiling of the Sistine Chapel by trial and error. If one of them couldn't invent the operators needed to move DRock1, it wouldn't matter who was right or who was wrong. Earth was doomed.

Autumn looked over at her officemates. Emila now crouched in a kneeling chair staring at her display and Fielder's back undulated while he chewed on his jerky again. Each occasionally swiped their screen with brush-like strokes, altering the swirling images on them in subtle ways. Instead of their fighting, she wished she could expound on the rules of quantum field theory. No, not expound, but pound the travesty of the rules into their heads. The answer to every problem was infinity and it made her furious. There was no easy way around this and she had to resort to the ridiculous method of trying to paint on her screen one set of operators after another, until it worked. Except, her knack for it had reached another level. She had moved leaves into a pile. She knew what she would do next. She made a fist and hammered her desk.

"Autumn?" Emila said.

"Are you sure you're not fighting with Mack again?" Fielder asked.

"It's Makani. And, no."

"Then what's up?" Emila chewed on her thumb, glancing several times between her display and Autumn's. "You're running a program called Pyramid Power? What's that?"

"A lesson," Autumn said.

"A lesson?" Emila and Fielder said together.

"Never piss off a Quantum Witch."

* * *

A text from Autumn came in. It said:

Wait for it.

On cue, the secure phone in Makani's pocket buzzed. This sent him scrambling to his tiny smart-car, the perfect cover for the trip to the airbase to receive orders for his next recon mission. How could Autumn know about this? Maybe he should listen to her more.

* * *

Emila and Fielder stood by their stations. The bosses' faces appeared on the liquid displays.

Autumn stepped onto her wooden crate. Her coworkers and bosses had never listened to her in any meaningful way. No one did. Now *someone* would. That's why she'd done it. That's why they'd have to listen to her now. She began, "I want to bludgeon the vacuum state of the universe with an annihilation operator, not build castles in the cosmos." The fact that a poster on the lime green section of the wall behind Emila showed exactly that, didn't help.

She called up the feed to a display panel that had dropped down from the ceiling. "See this photo? Makani took it an hour ago."

Fielder turned. "Yeah, another desert. So what?"

Autumn clicked a remote to zoom in.

104

"I see the Sphinx," said Emila. "I'm with Fielder on this. So what?"

Then Autumn showed a second, older photo of the Sphinx with the three pyramids behind it.

"The pyramids are missing in the first photo?" one of the bosses asked to confirm the obvious.

Autumn clicked again. "Here's one from the M1 satellite showing them on the Moon."

"Fake news," Fielder said. His whole body started to twitch like he'd narrowly missed being side-swiped by a semi-truck.

"In this case," Emila jumped in, "that's the most believable explanation." She started to fidget like she needed a cigarette.

Autumn put on the look of a perplexed teacher. "That's because most people have never heard of the Reeh-Schlieder Theorem, or even its common name, the Taj Mahal Principle."

"No, most people haven't," Emila agreed. "But if you'd moved the Taj to the Moon, that would get noticed."

"That would have killed people." Autumn was mad, but she wasn't murderous. "It doesn't matter who else believes these photos are real—it's starting to dawn on you what I can really do. Next time I'll drop the pyramids on our heads unless you listen to me."

"Didn't you just imply you were worried about killing people?" Fielder asked.

Autumn ignored them and turned to the mason jars. "Did you know apple seeds contain cyanide and uncooked kidney beans contain a toxin call PHA? And their taxonomic names sound like malicious and vulgar—so fitting. You two argue and I count. But this has to end."

"What?"

The room erupted with protest and confusion from her coworkers and the bosses. Had Autumn gone mad?

What did this have to do with moving the pyramids, or DRock1?

"Shut up!" Autumn's yell pierced the air and she cracked the crate with a stomp.

Emila, Fielder, and the bosses' chatter cut off mid-sentence and they eyed Autumn.

"Don't you get it? The seeds on the left are just as poisonous as the seeds on the right."

* * *

Makani made another pass over the space where the pyramids had been.

He didn't like politics, but called himself a centrist, when asked. Autumn, raised on a commune in California, liked to say he was a liberal like herself, even if he worked for the intelligence community. "You're just more sensible than my parents," she'd tell him. "And you're less sensible than mine," he'd reply.

Autumn explained she was a scientist. She liked to think about things and think things through. She liked to examine the evidence. But outside of objective studies of the natural world, she liked to balance the forces of freedom versus equality, to infuse the arguments with degrees of equity and fairness. She believed in compassion and empathy, and that everyone needed the chance to learn from their mistakes.

That's why he liked her.

He made another pass and zoomed in. The compact soil made sense, the outline of where tons of blocks had pressed for tens of centuries clearly visible. There were passageways to underground chambers. But there was also a glint. Something metallic. Something strange. He zoomed in further. There was writing on a large plaque. He took another photo.

* * *

"Next time I'll drop the pyramids on our heads unless you listen to me," Autumn repeated. With their rapt attention, she continued, "Don't you wonder if Earth is worth saving?"

"We're here to move DRock1," Fielder said.

"What else should we do?" Emila asked. "Let everyone die?"

"Don't you ever want Emila to die?" Autumn asked Fielder.

"Never."

"Don't you ever want Fielder to die?" Autumn asked Emila.

"Sometimes." Emila threw up her hands, as if to counter the shocked look on Fielder's face. "Well, you can be a real asshole."

"Autumn," one of the bosses said. "If you can move the pyramids, we can call off the tests. We don't have to move a mustard seed out here in the desert. Clearly, you can move anything, safely."

"You're a wonder," another boss chimed in. "You're an artist. You can move DRock1. You can save us. Let's not argue. Let's get on with it."

"No," Autumn said. "Every day I come in here and paint operators on my display, practicing quantum magic. But underneath it all, I know there's a fight brewing between the only two other quantum artists in the world that can save Earth. So, to let off the pressure you invented Freedom Friday. But that only confirmed my worst fear. Emila thinks she's on the path to equality and Fielder thinks he's on the path to freedom. But you're both on the road to hell." Wound up, Autumn continued. "Freedom and equality *are* the cornerstones of justice, but not if they are only propped up by the politics of grievance and blame. They must be balanced properly." She'd thought about saying that and everyone nodding. But her coworkers just stared blankly. Now pain entered her voice, as if she were mourning a loss. "I'm sick of all the fear and hate in this world, the reality of it all, the theater of it all, the emptiness of it all. Fielder wants to ignore the suffering of others and Emila wants to punish anyone that doesn't toe the party line. Instead of repeating slogans a gazillion times in our own vacuous lives, can't we try for real solutions, solutions that depend on empathy and forgiveness? I want to restore hope to this world, before saving it."

"We all want that," Emila said.

"We do," Fielder said.

"Save the Earth first," the bosses said. "Besides," one of them continued, "we'll fire Emila and Fielder if you want. Clearly, we don't need them anymore. We just need you."

"No, I don't want anyone fired. Didn't you hear what I just said? I want people to be able to learn from their mistakes." Autumn took in a breath. "Here, we are trying to move a speck. But we've forgotten to ignore the speck in our sibling's eye, while there's a beam in our own. In every religion there is a version of the golden rule. I learned that on my commune. Whether it is, treat others like you want to be treated, or, do not treat others how you do not want to be treated—the basic moral principle is the same. To live in the best of all possible worlds, we have to be good to each other."

Just then a text with a photo from Makani came in. It said:

Look at this.

* * *

In her writing room, Autumn set her note pad on the wooden crate beside her and thought about how the photos had changed everything.

For one thing, Makani had gone out of his way to listen to her, for a while.

She persuaded him to convince his parent to move to California near hers, and neither set of parents interfered in their lives. She and Makani moved into a comfortable home, surrounded by trees and gardens, where she could wall herself off from the world.

On a more major level, the last photo had changed the entire world, for a while.

Autumn opened her book.

It was the one she'd written to explain it all. The one that gave her the financial means to stay out of the fray, but which also helped her feel some hope.

She began to read the preface:

> Underneath the largest pyramid was a plaque made of a metal never forged on Earth. Its isotope signature showed it was alien. Carved into it was a message in the language of the local civilization, which described how the aliens had instructed the people of Earth to build pyramids, knowing these would hide and preserve the plaque for millennia.

> The message also described the galaxy and millions of other civilizations.

> However, the aliens behind the plaque were the first to master operating on the quantum vacuum. They saw the potential and moved their ships throughout the galaxy millions of years before any other species had left their star systems.

> But the aliens behind the plaque also saw the need to stay hidden. Thus, after finding an inhabited world, they would wait until identifying a group to instruct and then oversee construction of an artifact to preserve a plaque, before returning home.

> They would give no clues about their location.

> Finally, the message also contained a WARNING: the people of Earth must never travel into space beyond the pull of Earth's sun. If any signal from Earth were ever detected showing interstellar travel, the aliens would move the Earth. More precisely, they would drop

the Earth into its sun, incinerating it like a speck of dust tossed into a glass-blower's oven.

This warning on the plaque corresponded to the one the aliens left for all the other civilizations throughout the galaxy. It was their way of protecting themselves from the same fate once other species learned how to move pyramids, or an asteroid, ... or an entire planet!

This was the Great Filter. This was the solution to the Fermi Paradox. It was the reason we, the people of Earth, find ourselves alone.

It was also the reason the people of Earth stopped fighting, for a while.

And that was the reason Autumn saved the Earth.

(Well, there's also the fact Autumn considers herself a kind and decent human being. And also, she likes Makani and wanted to live with him for a long, long while.)

Ever since, it is one more reason we must listen to our fellow humans.

It is one more the reason Autumn doesn't want to remain silent.

It is the reason why we must not forget the lessons learned.

Autumn hopes that we listen to all the seekers of wisdom, to all those that yearn for freedom and equality, fairness and equity, truth and justice, peace, love and understanding; that we balance all the words and works of all the good persons and respond with empathy, compassion, and forgiveness, as we journey together on this rock called Earth.

— from Autumn's Almanac on the Day She Moved the Pyramids to the Moon.

Autumn closed the book.

It was a bit preachy, and she knew she had no power to make anyone listen to her since leaving the lab.

She also knew that none of the teachers, preachers, philosophers, or writers that had come before her had ever succeeded in achieving universal agreement on, well, on anything. No free and equal society could do that; any coercion achieved the exact opposite.

But while she was in the limelight (or, thinking of the control room wall, maybe lavender and limelight) she wanted to have her say. She would keep writing—even if she had to look around the beam in her own eye to shine a light on the specks that trip us up on the path to a brighter future.

AND MARVIN IS WATCHING

*— What does it take to find another person in a world
of great expectations?*

It's 1:00 pm Saturday afternoon and Marvin is watching.

A young woman opens the plain door of her apartment and steps into a common hallway. The caramel-colored cross-hatched soles of her red running shoes are like crushed ice cream cones, with the bright canvas like the ice cream dipped in strawberry sauce, and the ruffled tube socks like the whipped topping piled high. Against the worn and frayed tapestry pattern on the carpet underneath, the fantasy cone is enticing and clearly needs saving. Though Marvin tells himself he's just hungry.

Scanning upwards, Marvin sees the woman is wearing a pair of grey sweats—very clean. Behind her legs, the cracked yellow plaster wall looks like a Mercator projection of an eggshell with the yoke dripping out. Except, it seems the yoke is dried glue on the wall. But why was something glued to the wall so close the floor?

Marvin sees the woman's hips now. They're slender but rounded. Emerging above the drawstrings of her sweats, a violet nylon top moves skintight over her flat stomach and firm breasts. Yes, hungry, Marvin thinks, as the intended sexual rush hits his veins.

She has a happy face, like someone who has licked the peanut butter jar to the bottom. So happy, if you stood next to her, you'd look in the mirror to see if any of her happiness had smeared off onto you. If she's felt life's pain, she hides it well.

A statin scrunchie holds back her voluminous hair that seems eager to get free. Her makeup is perfect, so maybe she's running to a date. Marvin wants to be that date. If only he could meet her.

A young man enters from the foyer through a heavy oak door that has a three-by-three matrix of rectangular windowpanes. The one in the lower right is cracked. He walks beneath a grotesque baroque chandelier with tarnished minotaur-shaped figures twisting out of the brass, shooting arrows at water nymphs. He's clean-shaven, and his smooth skin matches hers. But his dress shirt is disheveled and untucked, and his long brown tie flaps over its buttons. He adjusts his belt and tucks his shirt into baggy brown pants. The brown plastic rims of his glasses frame his eyes. He seems slightly nervous, but harmless.

"Hi," he says to the young woman. "My name is Kenneth, um, Kern, ... uh, Ken. My name is Ken. Did you just move in across the hall?"

"Yep," she replies. "Bye." She bounds through the heavy oak door, through the foyer, through a set of double doors, down two steps, onto the sidewalk, turns right, looks over the hedges into the picture window of her apartment (an obviously new feature looking rather odd on the façade of the old building) and begins to jog parallel to a wide boulevard past a seemingly endless row of similar townhouse apartments lined up like dominoes. If one of those houses were to fall, they'd all come tumbling down. She fades into the distance while yellow cabs start and stop like pieces on a board game.

Inside, Ken stares at the door to the foyer. He turns to the door of his apartment and inserts a key. A heart with an arrow through it has been scratched into the wallpaper. Next to this someone has written in pencil, 'The geeks shall inherit the Earth.' Ken shrugs, opens his door and disappears into his apartment.

And Marvin is watching.

* * *

It is later in the day, though for Marvin it seems like only seconds have passed. He sees across a busy street into a shop. The chipped red letters on the rusting sign above the display window spell out SS Hobbies. The store is obviously of an older species, barely hanging on.

Inside, Ken looks about the shelves. A clerk approaches. At first Marvin feels like he's watching him through Venetian blinds, as white slats obscure his view. But soon it becomes clear he is watching Ken through the ribs of an enormous wooden model of a Tyrannosaurus rex.

"Can I help you?" the clerk asks. He lets a puff of air pass between his slightly parted lips, making a distinct 'ppha' sound.

Ken looks a bit haggard. "I can't find it," he says, swinging his index finger wildly back and forth along the shelves as if its frantic motion explains what he wants.

The clerk is a tall, thin-faced man with pitted skin and a narrow mustache that twitches like a marmoset receiving electroshock therapy. "Pray tell, ppha, what can you find not?" he asks.

"The TXE Super-trivia Robot," Ken says. He tries to not sound ridiculous. "I've been to sixteen-odd places, and they're all sold out. Now—"

"How many places, ppha? Is it what you want, ppha?"

"Er ... what? I mean the EXT. I got the letters backwards, the EXT Super-trivia Robot. It talks. It runs a trivia quiz ... uh ... for kids. I—"

"One person's trivia is another person's life's work, ppha," the clerk interjects.

"Yes, yes, I'm sure it is. I saw one in a box in your window, but I can't find it in here. I've been looking all over—I mean sixteen shops, really. If you're sold out, I'll take the one in the window. Just name your price."

"Would you consider Michelangelo's painting of the sixteenth chapel trivial, ppha?" The clerk's moustache ripples with a wave.

Ken moves toward the front of the store, passing the T-Rex. "Sistine Chapel," he mutters.

Through the plate glass display window Marvin sees Ken reach in among the neatly tiered shelves of model trains, radio-controlled WWII fighters, and drones. Ken grabs the box with the EXT, leaving behind a bright yellow, irregularly shaped star swinging in the window. In the star are the letters POW in a comic book font, advertising that the EXT is packed with action. But Marvin gets the feeling that something is not quite right.

Ken, clutching the box, find himself pressed between the display window ledge and the hardened face of the clerk. The T-Rex looms over the clerk's shoulders. The steel wing-nuts holding its wooden bones together gleam in the light. Rex seems to be smiling with a row of crooked, sharp teeth. But the focus returns to the clerk's face.

"Are you Sechzehn, ppha?" asks the clerk.

Ken's eyes dart to one side. "Sex-zane? Sex? Uh ... six? Oh, sixteen. God, I'm not sixteen. I'm thirty-four."

"Impossible, ppha! You cannot be thirty-four, ppha. I'm thirty-four!" The words boil off the clerk's upper lip.

"Thththirty-four." Ken gets his reply out slowly. "Can't we both be thirty-four? Why, it happens all the time." He laughs a little and gives a hopeful look. But the clerk's face remains in the solid state. "In fact," Ken continues, "probability predicts that in a room of twelve or more people the odds are better than fifty-fifty that two people will have the exact same birthday. Of course, that's not the same as the same birth year, or being the same age, uh—"

"Facts and figures, ppha. I should have known. How are you named, ppha?"

Ken is obviously too worried by the clerk's behavior to say anything.

"Your name?" the clerk asks sternly.

"Look, I'm a ... I'm a reporter with the Times. It's my nephew's birthday tomorrow and I'm late for work. I just want the EXT. What do you want for it?"

"Demonstration only for that model, ppha. Here, give it hererrrrrppha!" The clerk's pores look ready to erupt. He raises his arms.

"I'll give you a hundred dollars, no problem. Two hundred."

"It is for sixteen!" The clerk screams as he struggles to take the box.

"Fine, sixteen dollars it is. For goodness' sake, can't you accept a bribe?" Ken pulls the box back from the clerk's grasp.

Then they become visible, the clerk's cufflinks. So ominous is their jangling, cold sounds fill the air. They appear ten feet high and their shape becomes unmistakable: crosses with their arms bent into swastikas.

The image carved into Ken's retina's must send a rush of terror into his forearms with the speed of a bullet train. Marvin imagines the sound of wheels screeching to a halt and sparks flying beneath Ken's skin. But the screeching is coming from the fluted lips of the clerk as he is thrown into the T-Rex. In fright, he inhales his thin cheeks into his mouth while the model dinosaur's head begins to tip. Only now is it apparent how heavy those white lacquered bones are. As Mr. T tumbles down, for a moment Rex's collar bone is connected to the clerk's jaw bone. Then the whole head of the Tyrannosaurus falls, driving the clerk's coccyx to the floor with a thud. The clerk looks like a punctured puffer fish through the T-Rex's pearly whites.

Ken wastes no time. He bolts out the door with the EXT under his arm like a football. Marvin's view of this is from the street again, but he knows all that has happened. Back in the store he sees a short, bald, bull of a man with almost no neck come to the clerk and kneel. The clerk is hissing, literally.

"Sss, get him, ppha, sss," the clerk orders. "He has the EXT. Destroy the EXT, Achtundzwanzig."

"Yes, Vierunddreissig," grunts the bull-man.

And Marvin is watching.

* * *

City buses, taxicabs, vehicles of all kinds flash by in a whirl of color.

The city is a jungle. But where is Ken? Where is the EXT?

Marvin sees it is sitting on a blue plastic seat next to haunches wrapped in an intricately patterned dress, which is revealed to be worn by an older woman wearing a peasant scarf on her head and wooden shoes on her feet. Together, the EXT and the dress's wearer bounce with the beat of the bus, until brake squeals are heard. Ken comes up the bus's steps with the EXT under his arm and drops some coins into the slotted pillar next to the driver. It's clear now that the EXT next to the woman is not *the* EXT but another EXT.

Seeing the other EXT, Ken gives a slight squint of pain. He passes by it and finds a seat near the back, one that faces the aisle. The bus pulls away and Ken heaves a sigh of relief.

Of course, if only the bus had a window at the back, Marvin thinks. Then Ken would see what he sees. The bull-man standing in the bus's exhaust fumes, beads of sweat sliding over his flared nostrils emitting noxious gasses of their own. But then again, Ken doesn't know about the bull-man.

* * *

The city. Why didn't anyone cry, "Stop!" But the people kept coming, for jobs. The building kept rising, reaching for the gods. The townhouses so close together, with no room for trees, made of brick and grime for hearts seeking gold while pumping factory slime.

Why did so many people come to be alone? For the good city show, so popular it's now standing room only? But the *show* has been cancelled. The people are now stuck with no place to go. Stuck and caged.

Ever notice how animals in the zoo keep their posterior toward the visitors? Only those with catatonic glazed eyes look at you, but they don't see, anyway. Saddest of all is the lone primate who never gets to groom, howl, or grin at another of its kind. Don't the cagers know that a rocking cloth mother is as important as a mother's milk?

Then there are the pacers. Some primates pace for ten minutes waiting for a bus. Others pace for a lifetime.

Take, for example, Primate Smith pacing in his living room. Primate Smith has never met his neighbor, Primate Jones, who has just bought a new car. Hark, a way home from the *show*. Except, dammit, Primate Smith now has one too. So does everyone else. Trapped again!

How did it happen? It wasn't intentional. The rate of change began slowly. But try watching a beautiful, brazen autumn leaf rot and turn to dust.

"We have time-lapse photography, now," cries Primate Smith. "Those poor fools in the nineteenth century didn't know too many rats in a maze spoils the coup."

The coup?

Yes, yes, the Coup de Ville convertible stuck behind the bus with Ken, an EXT, and *the* EXT. It's a traffic jam, for better or for worse. But not for the car's driver, suited for business, not for patience, kneading his horn like it's made of clay while translating the comic strip hieroglyphs, #, $, %, &, *, into English words.

So, it's not hard to understand, with the bus standing still amongst all those cars clogging the city's arteries, how the bald bull is able to catch up to the bus, rap on its door, and gain access to its interior.

And Marvin is watching.

* * *

Sitting across from Ken is a pink girl. She's a 90's girl. Pink plastic sunglasses hide her eyes. Pink cushions on her mp3 player's headphones hide her ears. Her hair, shaved on the sides, is dyed (what else?) pink. Her lips sparkle with glitter immiscibly mixed into her pink lipstick. Her pullover sweater is bespeckled with pink buttons. Her blue jeans (no, they're not pink) are so tight the microbes on her pink skin are crushed, and run straight down her legs to her pink pumps, exposing a network of youthful pink veins. She sees no evil, hears no evil, speaks no evil.

Evil has just gotten on the bus.

Evil doesn't stop to put coins in the slot. Evil grunts and scans the bus. A funny thing must occur to Evil: it doesn't know who it is looking for, only what. And Evil sees it.

Rushing like a bull for a matador's cape, Evil pounces on the EXT. He throws the box with the high-tech toy to the floor, then with almost acrobatic grace he leaps into the air. Appearing to move in slow motion, his knees pull up to his chest, his boot bottoms hover like two potato mashers at the top of their motion, while his bald head points down the aisle. Ken sees this and hides his face behind an elbow. Other faces turn in horror, curiosity, or surprise—all except that of the pink girl. Her head remains fixed, implying that her hidden eyes remain staring into nowhere.

With ferocity, the boots come crushing down. Mass destruction takes place, and parts of the EXT fly out during repeated stomping, as it is torn apart, gear by gear. Finally, it and its box are completely demolished.

Everywhere there are looks of shock, except from the pink girl. Everywhere there is silence, except from the peasant woman, who removes a wooden shoe and begins bludgeoning the bull-man, cursing him in her own tongue. Ken pulls into the fetal position, but peeks as the bus driver pulls into a stop. The driver flees, either to get help or to save his life. It's unclear.

Meanwhile, the Coup de Ville's driver continues to knuckle the car's horn and curse as the EXT assassin moves along the side of the bus. Reaching the car, he grunts and yells, "Shut up." The car's driver responds with a wide, fake smile. "We sound very angry today—don't we?" The bull-man replies with a sharp blow to the Coup's windshield. It shatters. Tiny shards of glass fall, like teeth, wiping the smile from the car driver's face.

And Marvin is watching.

* * *

Hhrrrrrip. Hhrrrrrap. Hhrrrrrip. Hhrrrrrap. Hhrrrrrip. Hhrrrrrap. Marvin plays with the Velcro strap on one of his football gloves. There is something soothing about the sound of Velcro ripping apart and wrapping together again. Perhaps a mother's muffled heartbeat sounds like this. Or maybe ripping satisfies our need to tear the world apart, and wrapping satisfies our need to put it back together. Marvin ponders these things and wonders: how many times has his own heart been ripped apart—how many times has he had to wrap it back together?

* * *

Not far from Marvin, he sees the newsroom of a newspaper office.

The continuous clicking of fingers on plastic keyboards play a requiem for typewriters past. Cursors skip across screens leaving pixelated letters behind like breadcrumbs showing the way home while intense faces stare at trails of words and fluorescent lights crackle overhead.

Between glass partitions built upon waist-high wood-paneled walls, Ken moves to the newsroom. He enters a glass door and crosses between two rows of computers. One temple of his glasses is now held together with tape.

"Ken, hi," says a voice from behind a monitor. Two eyes, flanked by shaggy hair, peer over it.

"Um ... h ... hi, Pete," Ken replies. He continues on through a wooden door with the nameplate: Susie Watanabe, Life Styles Editor.

"Ms. Watanabe—sorry." Ken takes a deep breath. "Sorry, I'm late. I know it's past deadline, but I've had a day you won't believe."

"That's the third deadline you've missed this month, Ken." Ms. Watanabe, looking self-assured but friendly, leans back in a classic leather chair with her arms resting in her lap. Her white top and blue pantsuit fit together perfectly.

"I ... um ... know. But I think I've come across something of real value to this paper. I was looking for the TXE ... er ... the EXT Robot for my nephew—it's his birthday tomorrow—and the clerk—strangest little man you'd ever meet—well, actually he's rather tall—he, the clerk wouldn't sell me his last one."

"Ken, I know it's be rough since your last breakup."

"Oh, that. That was months ago. I'm fine now. But the clerk ... the clerk's a Nazi. The new kind, I guess."

"That's a pretty strong adjective for someone that wouldn't sell you a toy."

"But this clerk spouted gibberish, something about Michelangelo painting the sixteenth chapel. Sixteenth! I don't think it was a mispronunciation. But there was something else. He took an instant dislike to me, like, you know ..."

"Okay, maybe he's a racist. But maybe the breakup is still getting to you, and he was mixed up and you overreacted."

"No—he tried to take the EXT from me, fought me for it. I had to ... I, um ... I stole it."

"Stole it? How's that going to help the paper? What is this toy, anyway?"

"It's a robot, the EXT Super-trivia Robot. It talks and asks trivia questions on all the hottest topics, for kids. It's sweeping the nation."

"So, hasn't someone at the paper already done a story on it?"

"No," Ken says with more confidence than he's shown so far.

"All right, do a story about your toy robot."

"No, not about that. I want to do a story about the Nazi clerk."

"Ken, read the nameplate. Life Styles. Our readers want simple things that will improve their lives and glamorous stuff to dream about. Of course, if he was someone famous and a bit scandalous then—"

"No—but I was chased. The clerk sent someone after me, a bald guy without a neck. He found me on the bus and smashed the EXT into a mesh of bits and wire—only it wasn't mine. Mine was under my seat. He got a woman's by mistake. She was wearing wooden shoes."

"Destroyed it? Why?"

"I don't know. I was expecting him to attack me next—but come to think of it, I didn't see him in the shop. He probably hadn't seen me either."

"So, where is it?"

Ken looks at Ms. Watanabe like he's fumbled the ball. "Um, you mean the TXE ... er ... the EXT?"

"Yes! Obviously, it's important to them, so that's the key to your story. So, where is it?"

"Um ... I gave it to the woman."

"What? Whatever it was about this robot that made them want to destroy it, that's what you need to find out."

"I see ... I wasn't thinking. The woman—she looked so distraught. I, um ..."

"I'm sorry, Ken. Really, I am. But this paper comes out every morning, and it'd be damn boring to read if all the pages were blank. I'll re-run one of your columns tomorrow, but—"

"I was chased by a Nazi. Tomorrow's my nephew's birthday. Next week would have been the second anniversary of my first date with ... um ... you never met her, did you? Um ... I'm sorry, you're right."

"Ken, this is not TV. You can't expect to chase robots, Nazis, and a woman with wooden shoes, all while trying to solve your personal problems, and get your work done. I may have to let you go. For now, you're suspended, without pay."

"But—"

"But, I'll give you a chance—maybe a one in a million chance—but a chance. If you can find the woman, find the EXT, and it turns out to be something big, and I mean really big, I'll let you back on the payroll. In the meantime, I'll give the story officially to Pete. But I don't want him wasting his time on it. You do the work, and if it *works* out, I'll even give you a promotion and a raise. Contrary to the clichés, isn't that what life's all about?"

Ken nods and turns to the door, but pauses when Ms. Watanabe stops him.

"Wait. Before you leave, tell me, what happened to your glasses?"

"It was the woman ... she hit me with her wooden shoe when I gave her the EXT."

* * *

Hhrrrrrip. Hhrrrrrap. Hhrrrrrip. Hhrrrrrap. Hhrrrrrip. Hhrrrrrap. Marvin continues to play with the Velcro strap. It's a neurotic habit, he knows.

Outside the limestone front of the newspaper building Marvin sees Ken go down steps to the sidewalk. It's a less travelled part of the city and only a few people are about. Ken walks to a corner bus stop and waits. A bus comes and he boards it.

Suddenly it's apparent to Marvin that Ken is being watched. Marvin sees them: Evil Squared. The puffing, now hissing clerk and the bull-man sit in a black Mercedes with the bull-man at the wheel. The bull-man starts the car and follows the bus. Deep, regular hisses, like wind exploring a cave entrance, come from the clerk's cheeks. He's bitten them clean through.

And Marvin is watching.

* * *

Everyone knows misery loves company. So, it's not surprising that Ken is with Pete in a bar.

"Another gin?" Pete asks.

"Why, do I look depressed?" Ken replies.

"Yes, you do, and to fix that you've got to find her. But think of me. I'm supposed to write some silly piece about the impact of the EXT on trivia and culture, along with all my other work. At least you have the time to pursue something interesting."

"For free. And how am I going to find a woman I only saw for a moment, with her face obscured by a swinging shoe? I don't even know if there's anything *to* find."

"Don't worry. Watanabe is reasonable. She'll hire you back—if you turn something in. She likes your writing. She complains reading mine is going to break her back. You know, when she says she has to keep lifting the meaning up from my heavy prose. Not that it's my fault. I never learned to write for a sixth-grade mentality."

"Thanks a lot."

"I'm not implying anything. Don't be so sensitive."

"Sensitive? Ms. Watanabe thought maybe I had overreacted." Ken sips his drink and appears lost in thought.

"Ken, I'm not talking about putting up with Nazis. That's crap. But with women, you can't be too sensitive. Women hate that."

"But look at you."

"Sensitive? Me? That's my point. If I looked like the captain of a football team, like you do under those glasses and crumpled shirt, I'd probably do much better.

Looks are more important to women than they'll ever let on. But I was born with a bod destined for comedy. I've made the best of it. I'm funny, which means I can be sensitive. Though I'm sensitive in an assertive way. You see, our own idiotic Life Styles columns have brainwashed women to look for a sensitive man. But you can't ever show weakness. Underneath my sensitive act, when I get alone with the ladies, I show complete confidence. Unfortunately, that won't work for you. So, dress up and show off your body, and don't try my sensitive act. For you, act aggressive, like you're in charge. Right?"

"Right," says Ken. "I mean, you're right about some things. But in this case, you're full of shit." Ken raps the bar with his empty glass and leaves.

"Hey, don't be so sensitive," Pete says to the air where Ken was a moment ago.

* * *

Under yellow streetlights, Ken looks like he's moving through an alien atmosphere. Nightclub marquees flash an easily understood message that bright light is not welcome here. A drunk man clings to the fine wire mesh of a trash barrel bolted to a lamppost. Passing by, Ken glances at the man and the barrel.

Ken goes around the corner—but Marvin's attention is forced to pan back to an engraved sign on the barrel, which says, 'paper omnium.'

What a strange euphemism. What a strange trick to play when even a waste bin is given a more considerate description than the man beside it. Or maybe, if two respectable people walked past, one would remark, "Oh, look at the flesh omnium by the container for paper of all types."

Without warning, though not unexpectedly, two cones of light illuminate the reticulated pattern of the trash barrel, and vapor is seen seeping like a venomous mist from between the chrome slats of a Mercedes grill.

125

The car seems to absorb light, to vanquish good, to stake out the darkness like a hearse. Of course, in daylight it could turn out the car is covered in fuchsia polka dots. But that's not likely, given the swastika hood ornament. Around the corner the car goes, past the drunk and the trash barrel. Its occupants are certainly not contemplating the cosmic implications of a label such as paper omnium.

And Marvin is watching.

* * *

The eerie green glow of the interior of a bus moves like a hovercraft down a city street. The bus stops and lets off a passenger. It's Ken, who walks to the corner, his shoes tapping out the only sounds in the silence. He turns onto the boulevard of townhouses and stops in front of his own. Something stirs and Ken's nervous expression shows he'd rather not find the source. But his eyes scan the low-lying hedges lining the building's front, then search to his left along the curb of the wide sidewalk. Another sound is clearly heard now. It's a murmur, like the low growl of a big cat. Slowly, Ken turns around. First nothing, then intense light from two eyes leap upon his face. The Mercedes is ready to pounce.

With a roar, the engine is gunned and a black and chrome streak bears down on Ken. He seems unable to move, but jagged nerves must be sending out the alert. The Nazis are coming! The Nazis are coming!

Ken jumps as only someone up to their eyebrows in fear can jump. For a ridiculous moment he appears like a cartoon character who has run off a cliff. His arms flail as his legs retract while the car passes below. But Ken's momentum carries him over the hedge and with the tintinnabulation of breaking glass, he crashes through the picture window of an apartment and splatters onto its floor. Only moonbeams reflect off the broken glass next to Ken's face. His plastic rimmed glasses, now completely broken, hang like a choker round his neck.

And Marvin is watching.

* * *

A young woman in sweats and a violet nylon top, with a light on her helmet and keys in her hand, walks her bicycle up two steps, through the double doors, the foyer, the heavy oak door, and past the 'yoke-dripping' wall to her apartment. Entering, she pauses before letting out a small gasp and saying, "Oh, no."

A woman of action, she gracefully parks her bike, shuts her apartment door, steps into a washroom, and wets a washcloth, which she takes it to the man lying on her living room floor.

"Mmm ... oooh." Ken groans as he regains consciousness. He blinks his eyes and opens them. "Oh, it's you," he says.

"Did you have a nice flight?"

"Uh ... er, what?" Ken looks around the room as if expecting to find lost words hiding beneath the couch or behind the curtains. His blurred view comes into focus on a pair of paintings in the room, impressionistic in style, and only two feet off the floor. Then, looking up, the gaping hole in the picture window is seen. "I guess I made a wrong turn at Mars."

"I thought Superman always came in through the wall," the woman says. "Were you drunk or did you overdose on kryptonite?" She pats Ken's nose with the washcloth.

"Ouch, its sore."

"Did you break it jumping through my window?"

"No, a peasant woman broadsided me with her wooden shoes, today ... er, yester ... er what time is it?"

She points to wall clock, also only two feet from the floor, which shows five minutes after midnight.

"I'm sorry," Ken says. "Some maniac ran me off the sidewalk with a car. Apparently, I jumped right through your window to avoid him. I can't really remember."

"How'd you know it was a him?"

"What difference ... uh ... I, uh, know. That is, I think I know who was in the car. I, uh ... god, my glasses are broken." Ken sits up and points to the window. "Listen, I'll pay for that."

"Here, lean against this." The woman pulls the couch over. "Now, tell me what happened. I want to know everything." The enthusiasm in her voice is remarkable.

"I was buying an EXT ... a birthday present for my nephew. I ... uh ... never mind. You'd never believe me." The glum expression on Ken's face says it all.

"Why do people always say that?" the woman asks with genuine sounding curiosity.

"I don't know. But believe me—you won't believe me. Let me help you with this mess and I'll get out of your way." Ken moves to get up but the woman puts a hand on his shoulder.

"Whacha running away from?" she asks

"Uh, Nazis?" Ken clearly is trying to not sound idiotic.

"No, no, I mean, why are you trying to run away from me?"

Ken tilts his head and gives her a perplexed look. "Don't confuse me. Nazis want to kill me, people think I'm too soft—maybe in the head—and I've got to find a woman with a contract out on my face or I'm out of a job. Sorry ... I don't even know your name. I'll just get out of your way and let you carry on ... carry on with your evening routine, I suppose."

"Well, Kenneth, let's just say you've become a part of my routine. I'm very flexible. And, I know you've been wanting to meet me."

"You do? I mean, you know what I've been wanting? And you know my name?"

"I must admit crashing through my window is taking pretty drastic action. But as long as you're here, why not take the time to get acquainted? My name's Yolanda Wise. But my friends call me Yola."

"Yola, very nice. I like it. But how do you know my name?"

"It's on your mailbox, Kenneth Y."

"Of course. You're Y. Wise. The Y's caught my attention. I'm Kenneth Young, but I go by Ken. But, you know, you weren't all the flexible yesterday morning when I tried to say, hi."

"Oh, sorry. A friend really needed me ... my boyfriend."

"Oh." Ken looks down for a moment, then back up with his brave face. "So, Yola, what do you do?"

"I teach aerobics, yoga, and physics at the local community college. Now it's my turn to ask a question. What do you think is the most important thing in life?" Yola smiles at Ken with such a happy look, it's as if she's willing Ken to smile too.

"Boy, you don't give a guy a chance to catch his breath, do you? How about an easy one, like what my job is?"

"Nope. Let's skip to the good stuff. So, tell me, what's the most important thing in life?"

"Uh ... er, I don't know, a fulfilling job, a good family, maybe. Uh, what do you think?"

"Love." Yola waits as if the word will lift Ken from the floor. "When you're in love, none of the other things matter. I wrote a poem about it. Hollow Happiness/A shell we live in/It says to others, I don't need you/I'm happy without you/But you have to keep moving or the shell will crack/All it takes is letting someone in/Then you can throw away the shell and be born."

"I wanted to say love," Ken says. "I guess I was too embarrassed. I guess I was being silly. Then again, I guess it's easier to say love is the most important thing when you're in it."

"No, no, I'm sorry. I was being silly." Yola suddenly starts to cry. "It's only when you've lost love that you realize how important it is."

Ken looks distraught for a moment, uncertain what to do. Then he reaches out his hand. "It's okay. Tell me about it."

Yola puts her hand in Ken's and she lets out a choked laugh. "Oh, it's really nothing new. I broke up with my boyfriend last night. It's been a long time coming. And then, there you were, lying crumpled on my floor when I got home. It's strange. I used to think that to be born, marry, have children, and die was the most meaningless way possible to go through life; simple mindless perpetuation of the species. I wanted to strive for more. But I've found part of the striving is in the loving of another person. To share with another adds to the meaning. Really, it's the only way we can discover the truth about ourselves ... or perhaps this is just more silliness. What do you think?"

"Wow," Ken says. He seems stunned, his strong jawline underlining sensitive eyes.

Then Yola studies Ken's face and an unspoken moment occurs between them. She leans against him.

"Ken?" Yola finally asks.

"It's been a long time since I've met someone who's looked at me like you just did. It's been even longer since I've met someone who thinks about things."

"We all think about things."

"Yes, but we usually don't talk about the important ones."

"I guess the timing was just right," Yola says. "You've got me on the rebound."

"My breakup was three months ago. You've got me on the rebound too. Maybe I should say, you've intercepted my pass and I've intercepted yours. I'm more of a football person." Ken laughs. "But I'm glad."

Ken caresses Yola's hands and she pulls him closer, away from the broken glass. They hug and kiss.

"It must be very difficult for you," Yola says. She touches Ken's upper lip with her mouth. "How long were you with your girlfriend?"

"Two years. And with your boyfriend?"

"Five years."

Ken pulls Yola close and her breasts push against his chest. "It must have been very hard to leave him.

"Yes," Yola says. "They say ..." kiss "... it takes ..." kiss "... half as long ..." kiss "... to get over ..." kiss "... someone ..." kiss "... as the length ..." kiss "... of the relationship." She falls back and Ken moves over her, kissing her more deeply while her hands explore his back and farther down his body.

"My god," Ken says. "You mean ..." kiss "... I'm going to ..." kiss "... have to go ..." kiss "... through this ..." kiss "... for almost ..." kiss "... another year?"

"Agonizing, isn't it?" Yola kisses Ken more and more.

"Mmmm," moans Ken.

Ken unbuttons and removes his shirt, but the lights go out. "What happened?"

"Probably ..." kiss "... a power ..." kiss "... failure ..." kiss "don't you think?" Kiss, kiss, kiss.

More clothes come off. She removes his belt. He lowers the straps of her top, revealing her bra and pulls off her sweat pants with tenderness and ease. Then he kisses her flat stomach and works his way down.

* * *

It's amazing, the rich hues lovemaking adds to the darkness. It's as if one can see in the infrared, with wave after wave of warmth emitted from the lovers gently rocking silhouettes. The rich aromas, the feeling that nothing else matters, that all is right with the world. That's how life should feel—always. The afterglow that the act brings, the feeling of oneness, the closeness that means so much to those in love. That's what it's all about. At least that is what Marvin remembers from years ago.

* * *

The gentle moonlight reveals our two lovers, their silhouettes now under covers.

"Wow," Ken says.

"Wow, wow," Yola says.

"I hope you feel as great as I do." Ken sits up on his elbows showing his strong biceps. "I mean, I hope you felt ... um ..."

"The room shook." Yola isn't looking at Ken.

"You mean the Earth moved, don't you?"

"No, I mean just now. Didn't you feel it?"

"What?"

"There it was again." Yola puts her hand on Ken's shoulder.

"There's probably someone walking in the hall."

"You're probably right. It's just sometimes I feel a strange resonance oscillating in this room. I guess it's a psychological reaction to this place's past."

"Huh? What? I don't think I know about that."

"It's about the previous owner of the building. It's quite the story. You've noticed the pictures in here, haven't you?"

"I figured you spent a lot of time sitting on the floor, working out. You teach yoga, so that makes sense, doesn't it?"

"The pictures belong to the old owner. He was confined to a wheelchair and was very independent. But he was a loner." Yola pauses for a moment. "The story is the loneliness wore on him, caused what was human in him to wither and die."

"What happened?"

"One night," Yola says, "he rolled up and down the hall in his wheelchair with a shotgun under a blanket. As each tenant came out of their room and asked what he was doing, he replied he was a tank hunting for Germans. But he fell onto the floor and social services was called."

"Oh," Ken says. "Which room was his?"

"This one."

Yola and Ken remain silent, but there is a thud and the whole building shakes.

"Whoever that is, they're big," Ken says. "But it's an old building. Maybe we should call someone about the power. Do you have the time?"

"I can figure that out by the Moon," Yola says. She walks over to the broken window. "We have a great southern exposure here, except for the tall buildings farther down the street. By the way, there's a phone over there." She nods in the direction of an end table.

Then, in a collage of rapid-fire events, tension sweeps across the room. First, there's the click, click of Ken's fingers pressing for a dial tone. "That's funny," he mutters. Then Yola says, "Who's big car is that?" Finally, Ken turns to her and reacts in horror as the bald head of the bull-man eclipses the Moon.

"Yola, run!" Ken reaches for her and she falls back and stumbles into him.

Together they fall down then flounder to get back on their feet as two Nazis punch out the remaining glass and climb into Yola's apartment.

"Sss, we have you sss pphaa," says the clerk. He pulls a luger from his trench coat. But an explosion from outside echoes in the room, followed by the glow of flames behind the Nazis. They turn and gaze upon the burning Mercedes out in the street.

Quick as lightning, Yola and Ken bolt through the door.

"This way, out the back," Yola says. Ken joins her and they run down the hall, out the emergency exit and into an alley. Then they run, and run, and run some more, until they stop and pant in a small empty lot.

Ken exhales and looks up. He sees the clerk and bull-man coming up the street. The clerk is whipping the bull-man with a glove. Ken touches Yola's arm and points.

133

"Sweet mother of the universe," she says.

"Quick, hide," Ken says. He takes her hand and they move behind a dumpster. For a few breathless moments they wait while the clacking of boots passes by. Then they slowly head back toward the townhouse.

"Look," Yola says, pointing at the road. "Look at the asphalt. It's been torn up, as if a bulldozer—"

"Or a tank has been here. Yola, the old owner ... whatever happened to him?"

"He was put in a mental hospital. But I heard he was recently released. I didn't want to tell you that before, and, you know, freak you out."

"Yeah, that's not the kind of freakiness I need more of tonight." Ken's eyes meet Yola's and their slow blinks show his emerging confidence melting into her deep compassion. They are in this together.

And Marvin is watching.

* * *

On it rolls, so predictably. The lovers stroll through sunlit parks, play catch with cantaloupes in the market, and share a giant chewy pretzel, biting from opposite ends until their salted lips meet. But always they keep a wary eye.

"Do you think they're still looking for us?" Yola asks.

"I think I see them everywhere," Ken replies. Then Ken sees her, the peasant woman. He grabs Yola and they go in pursuit. But after catching the woman they learn the EXT is in the Netherlands with the woman's granddaughter.

Later, Ken and Yola discuss their next step, and she starts to wonder about his obsession with finding a toy.

"Are you crazy—go to Holland?"

"Why not?" Ken asks. He softens, turns to her, and says, "Think of it as a pre-wedding trip." His eyes are now moist and Yola can't resist. They hug and kiss, and kiss, and kiss, and kiss.

In the Netherlands the granddaughter reveals the EXT went out in the morning trash. She complains American cartoons lack the good sex and violence of American movies.

At the city dump the EXT is found, but the Nazis are there too. There's a long chase scene, but Yola and Ken escape and reach the US embassy. Agents reveal the EXT contains plans for a homemade dirty bomb and a New York subway map. But back home no one thinks the threat is credible. The map doesn't match any of the city's mass transit routes. Then Ken does a wider search in the library and realizes the map also has a code, and a timetable and tunnel near the Capitol building in DC is revealed. Fast forward, Ken, with an updated press pass, leads Yola to the bomb, which she diffuses with less than a second to go before it would have detonated.

After returning to street level, they find a group of Nazis have arrived. Yola and Ken are pinned down during an all-out battle. It's hopeless, last words are exchanged, but in the proverbial nick of time, a tank arrives—flying in from above. It's from an orbiting starship and it blows away the Nazis.

As the debris falls, a wedding scene is revealed. Ken, in a tuxedo, signs his name below a newspaper article. *Toy Hid Nazi Plans from the Future*, the headline says.

"Luckily, the wheelchair, tank-driver guy was from the future too," Ken says. He hands the newspaper to Pete and heads up the aisle to join Yola, who smiles at him, a beacon of grandeur in a fabulous dress.

Then Yola and Ken enter their new, lush apartment together, with beautiful paintings hung at the usual height. Together they kiss and fall onto their king-sized bed. The fan above whirls and sounds of love fill the air.

How perfect Marvin thinks, as the credits roll by. He leaves the theater and makes his way along the walk to his townhouse apartment, wrapping and unwrapping his Velcro gloves.

135

At his door, Marvin stares across the hall. He thinks about the young woman who lives there. He's never talked to her, never known what to say. Since graduating from college, he's found it hard to meet anyone. Maybe if he crashed through her window, they could start an adventure and fall in love. Would she expect that? But he goes into his apartment and closes the door. He flips on the TV and sits on the couch, alone.

And Marvin is watching.

THE MAN WHO FEARED DOING THINGS TWICE

– A young man confronts past heartbreak, the promised present, and a possible future.

When I enter the open-air bus, I'm struck by the old man at the back. I try not to stare and zero-in on a seat half way down the aisle. Soon we're off for the market.

We bump along the cracked and parched dirt road. The wheels kick up dust. It's terribly dry. I view the passing scenery through a brown fog as if it's a motion picture filmed in sepia. My face acts as a giant collector. Sand pits my skin. Beaches surround my eyes. I imagine my eyebrows sticking out like bushes from a dune. I feel disconnected, part of another universe.

I don't know what makes me turn around. Maybe it's boredom or perhaps an attempt to escape the dust. There. I catch sight of him. White. Reading a fat paperback book. Sitting in the last seat on the right. All in a glimpse, I see this.

White. That's what strikes me. In my first six months since coming to Promise I've rarely seen a white face. I glance again—and I'm about to look away just as quickly when something else catches my eye. A feeling of disbelief passes through me while I witness a most perplexing event. The old man, apparently after finishing a page, tears it from the book, crumples it up, and tosses it out the window.

137

I must be seeing things. I turn toward the oncoming dust but curiosity lures me back. Yes, it's happening. I notice the book has no cover. Pages are missing. I watch the old man finish the front and back of another page, tear it out, crumple it, and toss it out the window. Surreptitiously, I observe three more pages meet the same fate.

Life is weird. What I really want to know is, just how fat was that book before the old man had begun amputating its pages?

* * *

Time rolls on and we reach the market of Promise. The bus's tires etch their last bit of track in the dust. I exit in a hurry, not wanting to face the old man. Having to speak to him, even a passing hello, would be excruciating. He's obviously disturbed.

While walking to my hotel I think: there are two important things in life, writing and wild passionate love. Of the two, I'm more preoccupied with thoughts about the latter.

After I check in, I dash to my room like I have a consort waiting. In a way I do—her name is solitude and I desire to slip into her inky realm, to inhabit her unworldly haven. Once I'm behind the door, I set the deadbolt and slide to the floor. I'm like a teenager sneaking out of the house under a full moon, a criminal crossing the border into midnight, a lover leaving a stranger's bed before sunrise.

I sit, lights out. It's humid, but I keep the windows shut, the curtains drawn. I want to deprive myself of all sense of this world. I want the illusion I've entered a different dimension.

Alone. Alone. Alone. I want to feel it in my bones until they are bleached inside my flesh, my soul surrounding them like a desert's wind.

Deeper I sink into this state. The graininess on surfaces dance in the dim light. Shadows make the features of the room dissolve. I stare hard at the bed and it disappears. Time stops and my body stretches to infinity. Truth laughs at me and tears come to my eyes.

I feel empty.

"Did you really think you could find me here," Truth calls out. "Ha, you're so lost. You can never escape the past. No matter where you go—no matter what you do—I'll find you and crush you."

Next, I'm running in a maze. Every turn puts me right back where I started. Truth kept laughing and laughing. It is all in my mind, but now I start to cry and I finally let myself think about her.

Dammit, I always think about her.

* * *

I open my eyes and realize I'm in my hotel room.

I click on the light and reality clicks back into place as if I've just changed channels on the TV. I must have fallen asleep, because it's now dark outside. I have the horrible urge to go to the hotel bar and try to meet someone. But I've come all this way to try and write. So, I try.

Nothing. Nothing. Nothing.

I can't write, and I head to the bar.

* * *

My father drank in Mama's Tealeaf Tavern during my birth.

He chose Mama's because, hey, with a name like that it couldn't be one of those bars his mother had warned him about. Besides, he was searching for mothering. He ordered an Irish coffee, nursed it, and told the server about his royal ancestors, which he invented. Sorting out his actual past would've been like mixing all the flavors of powered kids' drinks in a bowl with water and trying to decipher the original flavors. He was a midwestern boy who made a lot of stuff up. Mostly he was goofy. But for some reason his flirting worked. He

139

left that night with a waitress in a frilly dress. Or so I've been told. I never met him.

My mother raised me. She taught me to respect women, which was good. She also told me women don't respect men who feel lust. So, when my first girlfriend in college dragged me to her room and undressed, I tried with all my might not to feel what I felt.

Afterwards, it wasn't a great moment. I thought I had used her, that she had enticed me because she felt the need to please me, or maybe she wanted validation, or maybe she wanted marriage. It was also my first time.

Three months later she left me for a guy, she explained, who didn't overthink things.

I then tried a more balanced approach. I told myself it's possible to lust and respect at the same time. Actually, my second girlfriend told me that. She definitely didn't like the scum that used bars like meat markets, but when she explained to me what she wanted, it wasn't all that different from what I wanted. We shared everything: our minds, our bodies, and our souls.

One day she left me too. My mother said it was because I cried in front of her, after seeing the first girlfriend at a party. That also wasn't a great moment. But girlfriend number two explained to me that my crying wasn't her reason for moving on. No, she said, it was simply that she'd always known I wasn't the 'one.'

That's when I *moved on* from my mother. While indubitably very clever, I suspected her understanding of relationships was highly dubitable. I finished college and, sans girlfriends, set out to become a writer. A lonely one. Writers are supposed to be lonely, right?

Of course, a twinge of guilt plucks a string inside me as I enter the bar.

* * *

Lust. Lust. Lust. It's doing aerobics in my arteries, hiding in my heart, longing to show its latent heat. It's

140

been five minutes since I took a seat in the bar in an empty booth. I'm sweating. My glasses fog up, but only due to the humidity. It's very hot here in Promise. Yes, that must be it.

"Hey brother, how's your wife? Er, how's your life?"

A young local man, my age with huge bushy mutton chop sideburns, grins at me and reaches his hand from across the booth.

I slowly reach back and shake hands. Where did he come from?

"You taking beer, brother?" he asks.

I notice he already has two glasses and a rather large bottle of Promise Pilsner. Before I can answer, he fills both glasses and slides one my way.

"Cheers," he says.

I slowly pick up the offered glass and take a sip. "Cheers," I say in an almost inaudible voice. I try to sound polite but not enthusiastic.

"So, friend," he says, "where you from?"

"America—the United States."

"Hah, big place. How do you like this place?"

"I find this place too hot," I reply. I notice his glass is empty.

"Too hot, this place." He's quiet for a moment, then asks, "What's your name?"

"Tom Bean."

He reaches out a hand. "Nice to meet you, Tom Bean." We shake again. "Very glad to meet you." His glass is full again. "You need to catch up." He points his chin at my three-quarters-full glass.

We sit in silence again while I sip more beer until my glass is half empty. Then I sneak a peek at the girls. When I look back, my glass is full. I take a few more sips but he immediately fills my glass.

"Do you live in town here?" I ask.

"No. I'm from that side."

I look at him, wondering if he'll indicate which direction that is, but he doesn't.

"I just come to town," he says, "to muck around, waste time. You know, there's not much work here. How about you people, plenty of jobs in America?"

"More than here," I respond. "But many people are out of work in my country too."

"You find people mucking in the streets like here?" His glass is empty, then full again.

"Some people sleep in the streets," I say. I keep sipping my beer, but I notice my glass never seems much less than completely full.

"So, are you on holiday?" he asks.

More beer comes, three big bottles.

"I'm here to try and write," I say. "I wanted a place where there aren't many tourists, but electricity. Someone at the airport told me about this hotel. It's quite nice. Who stays here?"

"Mostly government officials. They come to inspect the cane projects. I met one other European here once before. Only he had, what do you call it, blond hair."

"Yeah?"

"His name was Noland Buck, I think. We were very good friends. That fellow did everything. In two weeks, he can speak perfect Promise talk. He was very funny. We used to sit here every day, drinking, telling stories. He bought some jazz records and had a DJ play them here once. Told me about John Coltrane, and Alice too. Do you know them?"

"I've heard of them, I think."

"Uh, huh. That fellow, Noland Buck, had heard of all the jazz players. When he left, he said he'd send me some albums and write me every day."

"How long did he stay?"

"This place? One month, I think. We had a big farewell."

I see a bit of moisture in his eyes. Maybe it's due to the room's smoky haze.

"I hear he took one girl with him. I've got a picture. Want to see it?"

"Okay," I say.

He pulls out his wallet and shows me some small printed photos. "This one's my nephew, and that's some uncles at one wedding that side. And this fellow works in the home shop. Ooh, here's Noland Buck. He gave me this when we farewelled him, but I think he said this photo was from his schooling."

"Do you ever hear from him?" I ask. I feel more than a twinge of empathy. I hope for a positive response.

"You know, Tom Bean, this fellow, I write him ten times ten. But he never writes me."

More beer arrives at the table.

And on it goes. I sip. He fills my glass and empties his. More beer arrives. But he never lets me buy any of the beer, even when I offer. Another thing. When someone keeps filling your glass it's impossible to keep track of how much you've had to drink.

Soon it's midnight, the witching hour, with twelve bottles on the table. He says, "So brother, we go home?"

"Okay," I say. I stand up and prepare to go back to my room. "Nice to meet you."

"Oh, you're making a move?"

I'm not sure what he means, but I say, "Yep, time to go to sleep."

"Tom Bean, we'll have our supper first. In the morning we go home."

Now I'm confused. Then he pulls a rice sack from beneath the table and takes out something wrapped in paper. Supper. "Come, eat," he says.

I sit back down. "You're crazy," I say. But I start to enjoy my share of a wonderful Promise curry.

"Who's crazy, brother?"

"You. You're crazy, brother," I say.

He nods like this is a good name for him. "That's me," he says. "I'm Crazy Brother."

We're both pretty drunk. After eating I get up and walk carefully toward the door. I manage not to

GREGORY ALLEN MENDELL

stumble. The bar is empty except for one of the girls and us. She grabs me by the belt and says, "All night long."

"Okay," I say

She follows me. Crazy Brother does too. Back in my room we all lie on the bed, me on one side, Crazy Brother on the other side, and the girl in the middle. And we fall asleep.

* * *

There are two important things in life, wild passionate love and the meaning of it all.

What did life mean anyway? Are writers supposed to know the answer or at least try to find it? Don't writers who write with a message fail to reach anyone who doesn't think the same way? Don't they fail to learn anything new?

But why write if you have nothing to say? To entertain? Unfortunately, that takes talent. So, maybe it's the search that matters? Isn't it the search for meaning that gives life purpose?

What?

Blah! Blah! Blah!

That's better.

One thing, the answer isn't found by getting drunk. I'm fully awake now and my head is a mess.

And the girl is gone.

And Crazy Brother doesn't seem too happy. But he leaves after giving his sideburns a vigorous rub.

* * *

Later that morning, when I check my wallet, everything is there except my cash, which was forty dollars. I search for a shop that will take a traveler's check. No one knows what these are. Finally, after two hours, I find a place with stacks of tin plates in the window. After the shopkeeper tries to sell me teacups, bolts of cloth, and shampoo, he finds his father, who says he remembers using traveler's checks on a trip he took forty years ago, and he cashes one. He then points me to what he says every visitor in Promise wants, a greeting card to send back home.

Strangely, the father is right. I love discovering the punchlines, the quirky insights, the affirmations of love, the delightful, smirking, plucky animals dispensing wisdom.

Ooh, here's one. Two bears look through a magnifying glass at giant heart-shaped paw prints. 'It's bigger than both of us.' Love is bigger than both of us, of course. Here's another one. Two elephants hold each other's trunks atop of a high diving platform above a heart-shaped pool. 'Go for it.' Go for love, it means. Finally, two birds sit on a picket fence with their cartoon fur singed. One holds a heart-shaped burnt match. 'Are we playing with fire?' The question is: are we playing with love?

Love. Love. Love.

There are also others. A young woman with a pie in her lap says, 'You like the taste, don't you?' A young man holding a banana says, 'Yes, let's trade.'

Sex. Sex. Sex.

Love and sex. Sex and Love. These are the first greeting cards I've seen in Promise. I guess when you live in a village with hundreds of relatives, who needs a card?

More to the point, who in Promise would want to spend money on one? But, on the other side of the stand, I find a local woman looking at more cards. She's holding a rat and cuddling it. It's no big deal. But, I wonder, if some people substitute sex for love, do others substitute love for sex? It's unfair of me to judge. I'm sure this local woman has a hundred relatives to hug and a home full of children.

Then it strikes me. How sad is this? I'm alone in Promise looking at greeting cards.

I try shifting to another aisle and freeze. It's the old man. He's looking at cards too. But he just stares at them.

"He's been there all day," the local woman says while passing by me.

At the door she looks back at him and at me. I see myself from her point of view. To her, I'm just like him. And it's true. I'm sure the old man has no one to send a card to either.

* * *

After escaping the shop, I look for a place to eat. But before I can duck into a café, I hear someone call out. "Hey, boy." It's the old man.

After some gentle persuasion, he convinces me to come to his home. Do I go with him out of pity? I'm not sure. Maybe it's because he's the first American I've met in Promise. I follow him down a side street to a remote corner of town. There he shows me into a traditional, modest home. I think I pictured something more colonial, but he goes behind a bamboo curtain separating the sitting room from a kitchen and returns with cups of tea. He wears an open pinstriped jacket, a baseball cap, black shorts, dirty white sneakers with yellow knit socks, and a light brown bowling shirt with the cursive letters DTP written on a pocket protector, which holds the markers probably used to write the letters. He hands me a cup and we sit in hard wooden chairs. I want to ask about the bus, the book. I also want to leave. I keep quiet. But finally, I ask, "How long have you been here?"

He ignores this and pulls two oranges from a bowl of fruit. He presents them to me.

I see he wants me to pick one. So, I do.

"How did you decide which one?" he asks.

"I don't know. I didn't decide, I just chose."

"And I didn't decide to come here," he says. "I just chose."

146

Okay, he wants to play games. I need to get out of here as soon as possible.

"Now tell me, boy, *how* did you choose? Hmm? I've searched all the markets of this place for two such oranges—so similar, so equal—for just such a test. I presented you with two equal states. You chose. How?"

"I really don't know," I say. "They were the same so I hesitated for a moment and—I really didn't think about it."

"Ha! You hesitated. That hesitation, boy, is evidence for a trace of free will!"

Oh boy, I think.

"You doubt me? Okay, do you think it was fate? From the beginning of time, was it slated that, uh, ... what's your name?"

"My name? It's Tom Bean."

"Glad to meet you, Tom Bean." He holds out his hand to shake.

Clearly, he's been in Promise for a while. "Tom Bean is my whole name. My first name is just Tom."

The old man clears his throat with a harrumph. "The first shall be last."

Okay, that's it. No more talking. It's pointless. I silently sip my tea until I notice the old man is staring off into nowhere. His bottom lip trembles.

"For love," he says.

"Huh?"

"I came here for love. Never to know it again."

His words hit me like a punch.

"Right after graduate school I got married. That'd be 1951. Came home one evening and found a note. She'd left me for a man of Promise, it said. The man was confused, had come to American looking for acceptance, but found none. But he did find her and asked her to marry him so he could return to his homeland without shame."

"And you came here to follow her?" I ask.

147

GREGORY ALLEN MENDELL

"To follow her? Oh no, no, no. The man could have been from Mars for all I cared. I came here to escape, to never make that mistake again. I told my friends that my wife had left me for a Martian. You know what they did?"

"No, what did they do?"

"They laughed. They laughed until their bellies hurt. And not one of them had ever known love."

"Why not?"

"Why not? Ho, ho, because they were physicists. And so was I."

"You were?"

"Of course. Look here. See these letters." The old man points the letters DTP. "Know what these stand for?"

I shake my head.

"Drxzl, The Physicist," he says. "That's spelled d, r, x, z, l. No vowels. I've run out of names with vowels."

"Your name is d, r, x, z, l?"

"Today it is. Tomorrow it will be something else."

"Something else?" I nod like I'm captivated by this conversation, while hoping for an opportunity to excuse myself.

"Pay attention, boy. I never have the same name twice. Tomorrow I'll be Dpzzd or something. But never the same name twice. Never!"

Why did I come here? Maybe I can change the subject. "You know," I say, "I just broke up with my second girlfriend. I really thought she was the one. So, I came here because I wanted to get away too. It's like this—I feel like I'll never meet someone like her again." All of this is coming out of me and can't for the life of me think why. Except now, I'm thinking of her, and I can't stop. "It's like I'll never fall in love again."

"You never will," he says.

"No, don't say that!" I don't know why I'm trying to argue with him. I don't know why I told him about her. Why do I tell everyone about her? But I continue. "Think of all the lose threads of life that must catch each other

148

and become knitted into a friendship, then sewn and re-sewn to form love. It seems rare. But one must not lose faith in love." I take a breath, wondering why I'm so wound up. "Forgive me. I think of myself as a writer, sometimes."

"Forgive me. I think of myself as a reader, sometimes. What have you written?"

"Nothing."

"Good, then you can still write. But never write the same thing twice, Tom Bean. I read two books per week, myself. But never the same book twice."

Oh god, I think. But there's more I must say. "You love to read. The books give you something. But you can be like a book. You can offer something of yourself to others. And better than a book, you might find someone that can offer something back. If you offer love, you might find it."

The old man seems a bit disturbed. "You also get used by people."

"So what?" Then I say the lie I want to believe. "You can give all your love away and not lose anything."

Now he seems angry and shouts. "I lost something! I lost my soul!"

I can't stop myself. I repeat the self-help I've told myself. "Pain exists, but it's worth it. It teaches us how important love is to our survival. You can survive alone, but never really live."

"My pain has not been worth it. My pain has been my life."

"Your choice." I realize how insulting I must sound to someone so alone. Am I that mean? I try to reach for some empathy, but I see myself becoming just like the old man. I realize I'm caught. I'm trying to convince him, to convince myself.

"Was it my choice that I am a man who finds it hard to change?"

"You can change if you want to."

"Can you? Can you, Tom Bean? How did you choose the orange? How did you?"

"What?"

"Free will, it doesn't exist. Your consciousness can't control things. Forget Bohr and Copenhagen. Your quantum state, if that matters, is controlled by deterministic equations. Nothing collapses when you make a choice. You carry on with the rest of the waves that make up the universe. Ha, regardless of what emerges from any deeper level, reality plays out as it must. Listen to me, boy. We are just electrochemical reactions shaped by our memories. That's all we are!"

This was getting too heavy for me. But the old man continued.

"Therefore, to defeat the universe, to have free will, we must never do the same thing twice. We must never do the same thing twice."

I didn't have the heart to tell him he'd just said the same sentence twice.

"Never the same name, never the same book. Do you know how I avoid temptation?"

I knew the answer, of course. But he continued.

"I'll tell you, boy. I rip out the pages after I read them. Look! Do you see any books around here? No! I read a page and rip it out, never to read it again. Ha! I rip it out, never to read it again. Rrrrip and it's gone. Ha! I rip them out. I rip them out. Ha, ..."

* * *

I wake on the old man's mat after a twisted dream about ripping pages. Something hurts deep inside, like I'm an orange that's had the last bit of juice squeezed from it. But the dream was a vision of a possible future—not a determined one. It's a future that I can change, because I *choose* to learn—from the past and the present. I'm sure of that now.

I realize I've made myself a couple of promises.

The first is to get out of the old man's house. I hear him snoring in a bedroom down the hall and leave without saying goodbye.

I reach the main street. Freedom.

But Promise is not a place one enjoys solitude for long.

"Tst. Tst. Hey, Tom Bean, you come home?"

It's Crazy Brother. Of course. "Hey," I call back. I know I will soon be one if his very best friends. Maybe I'll even write him from the States.

But I also swear I'll keep a second promise—one that makes me feel alive again, ready to greet Crazy Brother, ready to greet the rest of my life.

Someday, I will love again! Someday, I will love again! Someday, I will love again!

THE IMAGINARY WIFE

— When a vacuum phase transition separates a longtime couple, how can they stay connected?

"You have a wife?"

The incredulous tone in my old classmate's question knocks me back to when we worked together on physics problem sets in the basement of Jackson Hall and I knew she saw me only as a friend. I had relied on her more than she had relied on me when we strategized the route to particularly tricky solutions.

Now she's on my screen, the prestigious Dr. Eshana Dubkey, and I need her help more than ever. But before I tell her why, I try to defend myself. "I've been married for thirty-five years." Then I add, "Sorry, I've kept up with your papers, but not with you."

"Reading papers sounds like you. But what about your vow to Vulcan asceticism?"

"That was cosplay," I say. Eshana gives me the slight shrug she always did whenever I made this excuse. "I've never felt more than *half* Vulcan." Eshana knows that I'm joking, though in the past, jokes like this never elicited the hoped-for response. This time she raises an eyebrow above stylish dark-rimmed glasses and switches her quirky lip bite to a thumb bite. Deep intelligence radiates from her face. But an image, which never should have left my thoughts, shakes me hard and I return to the current desperate situation. "The reason I contacted you is my wife. She's trapped and it's because of one of your papers."

Eshana's look changes to dismay.

I must have sounded like I've accused her of something. "No, no," I say. "It's not your paper's fault— it's not your fault. It's mine. I started searching for monopoles ... like you."

"I thought you went into quantum cosmology."

Has Eshana heard me say my wife is trapped? But a detour into my research is needed, in any case. "During my postdoc I worked on dark energy in the early universe. That's when I met my wife. After another postdoc and two decades on soft money at a cyclotron lab, I burned out. We moved to Alaska, somewhat on a whim, because my wife had read about spinning qivuit wool gathered from wild muskox. That worked for her and for once I had some free time. I thought about your quixotic search for what happened before the Big Bang, and ... and I set up a SQUID in our house. Now she's trapped."

"How can a superconducting quantum interference device trap your wife?"

"Your SQUID worked, Eshana." Then I pour all of my love for my wife, all of my fear of losing her into the most stupid sounding sentence I could never explain to anyone else. "The SQUID in our basement detected a hedgehog monopole."

"I never liked the name, hedgehog, as cute as it is. But you mean a topological soliton with three types of gauge fields from a GUT era shortly after the start of our universe?"

"Precisely," I reply. "The result was a disaster. The circuits overloaded and blew the coolant. When I ran away and went outside to scream at the phantoms of experimental science, half the house became engulfed in a bubble. Do you get it, what that bubble is?"

"I think so," Eshana says. "It's the universe killer."

"Precisely," I say, again. "The monopole nucleated a vacuum phase transition, and a bubble of true vacuum expanded from the heart of the SQUID. However, it swallowed only half the house, not the entire universe. And my wife was inside the house. She's inside the bubble!"

"She's inside it?" Eshana's eye's bulge with the fear. "Is she alive?"

"Yes."

"Matter is still coherent in the bubble?"

"Yes, I'll get to that. At first, I didn't know what was going on. I told her to come out. That was a mistake. At the bubble wall she reached her hand through and it snapped back, almost breaking her wrist. She collapsed in pain. We agreed she should stay put until I learned more."

Eshana thinks for a moment. "A lower vacuum energy, a smaller dark energy density, should also correspond to a change in the masses of the particles. How can this work?"

"That's why I'm counting on your help. What I know is this. The monopole at the center of the bubble is extremely dense and point-like, but radiating light. I've measured the refraction at the bubble boundary, and calculated the stress-energy. Inside the bubble, matter is relatively unchanged, but spacetime is dramatically different. As in some theories of the early universe, time is no longer only real. You know what that means." I'm not sure Eshana does. The theories I'm talking about are more like just-so stories, with no evidence, or even exact equations. But she nods and confirmed my worst fears.

"Imaginary time," Eshana says.

"Precisely," I say.

"Therefore," Eshana continues, "the square of the time differential is negative, changing this axis from time to space, and the spacetime manifold from Lorentzian to Euclidean. It's like the surface of the Earth, no start or end to it, only endless circles around it, until the wave function of the universe quantum tunnels to start ours. Though how real time works in quantum gravity, let alone if it's replaced with imaginary time, is a bit of a quandary."

"It's more complicated than that. Inside the bubble, real time also continues to exist. The bubble's interior is a 5D spacetime, with one dimension of real time and a 4D space, which is our 3D space plus a spacelike imaginary time dimension."

"Where is she now? Can you see her?" Eshana starts to scribble on a notepad.

"The 4D space inside the bubble is a 4D sphere, expanding and contracting along the imaginary time axis. The portion of the house inside the bubble moves with the cycles of expansion and contraction, and this motion causes its intersection with the real time, real space plane to shrink and disappear."

"If I understand, you're saying your wife experiences a 3D space, but she's moving back and forth along a 4th dimension of space, which is an imaginary time axis?"

"Precisely." I needed to stop saying that. "The first time I saw this happen I thought she was gone forever. But then the bubble reappeared as a dot which grew again and we could see each other before the bubble shrank and disappeared. The time between appearances is increasing and the duration of her appearance is decreasing. I now see her once every three days, and only for a few minutes. We pass letters to each other during these occurrences. And other things. I first passed her bandages and a sling for her wrist. I've since pushed a generator, fuel, batteries, and jugs of water through the boundary. The tidal forces damage things, like her wrist, which is better, but strong containers can survive. So far, she's survived. I've given her books and knitting too. She has things to do. But ..."

"But ... but ... but." Eshana mutters while writing.

I blink and my eyes sting. "But what's the solution? I need to get her out."

Eshana turns her notepad to the screen. It shows a sphere intersecting a plane. Offset from the plane is a stick figure labeled 'wife' that lies in a 2D circle around one of the sphere's poles, with the direction to this pole perpendicular to the plane. Next to this is the sketch of a hyperboloid and the words 'de Sitter space' and 'no way off.' Eshana looks at me with irises that seem to swirl around her pupils like accretion disks around black holes. "I don't know," she says. "But it's bad."

* * *

Dear Line Segment,

I tracked down Eshana, like I said I would. I told her everything that's happened. She doesn't have a solution yet. But she's working on it.

It's like that book I told you about, Flatland. I've pushed it through the bubble wall with this letter. That's what I'm experiencing when you appear and disappear. Your 3D portion of space is part of a 4D sphere that keeps intersecting the 3D plane I live in. I'm enclosing an explanation with a few diagrams I've copied from Eshana's notes.

Love,
Your Square

* * *

Dear Square-brain,

Don't call me a Line Segment. In fact, based on your diagrams, I'm shaped more like the hourglass diagram labelled de Sitter space, don't you think? But I'm much more than that, right? Please find my longer letter enclosed in the book I need you to return to the library.

See you again soon.

Love,
Your Hourglass

P.S. Seriously, as much as I like having all the time in the world to read, I'm scared.

* * *

After a week of brainstorming, Eshana is again on my computer screen.

"I've got it," she says. "It's not all of de Sitter space, but a portion of it. Your wife is free-falling with the expansion and contractions, intersecting the plane you exist in with each pass. Because of the free-fall, she has no experience of motion, and she's small enough to not feel tidal effects in the bubble. But the discontinuity in motion at the bubble boundary creates extreme g-forces. I have one question. How many days of water did you give her?"

"A week's worth?"

"And how long ago was that?"

"Two weeks."

"And how much water has she used?"

"Hmm, I think the jug is still mostly full. I've wondered about that."

"It's time dilation. I've got a metric worked out. A day for her is a week for you. There's a scale factor in front of the imaginary time axis, and it grows to an enormous size, greatly slowing time, causing an effective motion relative to the outside of the bubble that approaches the speed of light. Actually, the expansion rate of space itself can exceed that speed. In any case, during the expansion, your wife literally moves trillions of kilometers away from you. Luckily, when the 4D sphere contracts again and passes through the imaginary time equals zero plane, the contraction goes through a minimum and the relative speed becomes zero for a moment."

"So, she could hop out then?"

"She could, but I'm afraid I have some very bad news. The amplitude of the expansion is increasing. The next few weeks for her will become a year for you. And the time for you to see her will shrink to seconds. After that, it will be too late."

"What do you mean?"

"According to my calculations, after a few years for you, her disappearances will start to last tens of our years and months for her, and she'll only reappear for milliseconds. Eventually, she won't reappear for a hundred years in our time, though only a year for her, having moved many light-years away and back again. Then again, her air and water won't last nearly that long. Already, if she tries to cross the bubble boundary, the g-forces will kill her. She's as good as gone."

I lose focus and stare as if lost in a dark void. "My real wife ... now imaginary ... gone."

Eshana promises to work on the problem and we say our goodbyes.

Then I cry.

* * *

Dear Hourglass,

I'm meeting with Eshana almost every day now. She's clarified the situation. The details aren't important but this is: the time between your appearances is going to continue to increase and the duration of our seeing each other is going to continue to decrease. Time is moving much more slowly for you than for me. But it will be okay. We'll get you out. I'm pushing in more water, more food, more batteries, more fuel for the generator ... and more books and wool too.

Love,
Still Your Square

* * *

My Dear Square,

For me, the world outside my bubble changes. It's like a time lapse movie of the sky with the clouds flying past. Every day they fly past faster. It's like I'm seeing parallel worlds pass by. But halfway between my return trips to you I see things outside slow down and my bubble moves inside another house, like ours, but different. And through the windows the world outside that house is different too.

However, I have to tell you something. For some reason I feel drawn to that house, like I should try to get out and see who's there. But if I understand your letters, we'd then be separated by light-years along an imaginary axis, which seems far too real to me, and I don't want that ...

Do you remember the letter you wrote me after I sent you one of my favorite poems? You talked about how we met at the lake, your worldline to your physics workshop and mine to my writer's retreat were destined to cross, as you put it. You then went into some nonsense about wave functions and stuff I don't remember. But we both fell down laughing when I rolled my eyes so hard you thought they might pop off my face, and I showed you a clip of a cartoon where this happens.

After that you pretended physics and science fiction were your only two interests. Except you proceeded to quote your favorite lines from about fifty novels and I knew I wanted to hear more, to see you more often. You weren't so Vulcan then ... or later, after we met for a cartoon film festival ... or after you took me to the science museum and showed me particles spiraling in a cloud chamber.

I wasn't sure at first, but I sent you the poem about not wanting to miss out. And you wrote back about how particles, like those in the cloud chamber, were now bursting out of your heart whenever you thought of me. You said you knew then you didn't want to miss out on me.

Now, I worry you're not telling me everything about what's going to happen next.

Love,
Still Your Hourglass

P.S. You mentioned time. You must be spending a lot of it with Eshana.

* * *

My Dear Hourglass,

Your description confirms Eshana's theory. You're passing through parallel worlds that exist in 3D planes parallel to mine, but which are offset by a non-zero value of imaginary time from my plane where imaginary time is zero.

You're also exactly right. I have more to tell you. The truth is, it's not good. A day for you is now a month for me. Soon a few weeks for you will be a year for me. And then ...

I've been thinking about our journey together.

You're so smart, and you're so much better at giving to this world than I am. Everywhere we've lived you've reached out and made a difference to others while I've stayed in my own little sphere.

Also, I know it wasn't just burnout at the lab, but also climate change that drove us to Alaska, where I'll never really fit in. Though I was lucky, which is such a terribly, terribly unfair thing to say about what happened next, and the tragedy of the pandemic. But moving here and having to isolate gave us so many moments together. I wonder about others with kids and family they haven't been able to see. I know it's been hard on you, leaving all of your friends behind, and not being able to travel to see them.

Our whole journey together ... having someone to share a walk, a video, a book ... and the other thing (I see that smile on your face) ... it can sound trivial, but these moments with you have meant everything to me.

So, I don't want to talk about the time we have left.

I just need you out of there.

Our Love,
Squared

* * *

Dear Diamond,

You fly by so fast now I see your 'square' shape tilted, just as you drew on another diagram. Know that you're my diamond in this rough universe and I'm holding on for you.

I'm pushing the sweater I knitted for you through with this letter.

Like sands through this Hourglass, I'm forever yours.

Love,
Me

* * *

Dear You That I Love,

If we live to ninety-eight-years-old we're only half way through our marriage. I want that. I want those years with you. But I'll take whatever I can get.

Squarely Yours, Forever

* * *

"How do two people stay together?"

I guess it's time for Eshana to ask me a question like this. She's told me so much about her life over the past months. She has kids, for one thing, but has never met the right partner and has never married. She's a super scientist and a super mom, happy to not feel committed.

Luckily, she's told me, her sister babysat whenever needed before her kids were grown, and she did have a series of relationships.

"How do two people stay together?" She repeats. "You know, for thirty-five years."

"Lots of shared walks, videos, books, ... and the other thing." Even though I smile, I feel immediately embarrassed I've shared this private joke with Eshana, especially since she's opened up to me about her current lack of a love life. She does look good. I can't figure out why a million worthy suitors haven't beaten down her door. Somehow—maybe it's the glass of wine we're sharing—I tell her what I'd really thought during those problem sets.

"So, the other thing? That still works for you?"

Ah, I get it. She's deflecting the conversation back to the present. "We've always supported each other, and our experiences together have allowed us to became more and more open with each other. Let me just say, over time we learned how to take turns giving each other all the attention and affection we each need."

"Maybe I should come to Alaska," Eshana says. "We could try something."

Did I misread her deflection?

She pauses for a moment and then cleverly adds, "... to save your wife, I mean."

That snaps me back to my plane of existence, and I write my beautiful, wonderful wife about how lonesome I am.

* * *

Dear Lonesome Square,

I can tell you've developed feelings for Eshana. That's natural, I suppose. The situation *is* desperate. I'm feeling that way too. But ...

I've been able to talk to someone at the different house. I'll call him Albert. He's not afraid to take chances and thinks I should take one too. He says he wants me to try to get out, to see his world.

I do want out, and maybe things move slowly enough where Albert is that I can do it.

Please don't break me. Please hope I don't break.

Your Fragile Hourglass

P.S. I don't want to leave you, but if I do reach out to Albert, I won't see you again.

* * *

My Dearest Hourglass,

Eshana has a complicated life, and we've talked. She might come to Alaska so we can work more closely. But it's you I miss. I should have made that clear in my last letter.

No matter what happens, you're the one that I want and everything I've ever wanted.

I will always love you.

As for Albert. I want what's best for you.

Hopelessly Yours,
I'm Squarely On Your Side

* * *

Dear Hopeless Square,

I'm on your side too.

But Albert tells me in his universe people have learned to live peacefully together, and the life span has been expanded. Even my aging process can be reversed if I join him.

I do love you, but I have to make a decision soon. And I have to post this through the bubble now.

With All My Love,

Your Wife

* * *

Dear Timeless One,

Eshana has news. Her third grandchild is due. She's always had big family reunions and won't be coming to Alaska. Instead, she's sent me a book—about Niagara Falls. I'm pushing it through the bubble wall with this letter. Most importantly, in the book are notes with my plan.

With All My Love,
Your Husband

* * *

On the screen Eshana cheers me on. "You have a real wife, now go to her."

I climb into a rubber ball wearing a g-suit designed for space travel. The ball is like one described in the book, which went over Niagara Falls and splashed into the river below without leaving more than a few marks on its inhabitant.

Now, I start to roll along the river of time, seeking something far more precious than fame. I relax the tension in my chest and brace myself for the tidal stretching I'm about to experience. That won't compare to how my heart will rupture if I don't try this.

I call to Eshana, "I'm off." She's told me she'll make a quick trip to Alaska after all, but only to seal off my house so no one can follow me. Then she'll return to her kids and grandkids.

With a few dizzying rotations I burst through the bubble wall.

* * *

After almost two years apart for me and a little over three weeks for her, after recovering from two strained rotator cuffs, after a lot of catching up with the multiverse's most desirable partner, it's time for our next step.

"Ready, Hourglass?" I ask.

"Squarely, yes," she says.

We're about to roll into Albert's universe. The one where Albert has a boyfriend, I've found out.

"All's well with worldlines that end well," I say.

"May our journey continue for many years," she says.

"And may the other thing continue too," I say.

She smiles and rolls her eyes like the cutest heart-shaped dice one could ever hope to gamble with and win. I'm so lucky.

"A whole new lifetime, a whole new universe awaits us," she says. "It's like the end of the poem by E. E. Cummings I had framed for you when you left the lab, *pity this busy monster, manunkind,* don't you think?"

"Precisely," I say.

We hold hands and together we say, "Let's go."

GREGORY ALLEN MENDELL

STORIES

FURTHER READING

Something Deeply Hidden: Quantum Worlds and the Emergence of Spacetime by Sean Carroll; Dutton, 2019.

What Is Real? The Unfinished Quest for the Meaning of Quantum Physics by Adam Becker; Basic Books, 2018.

Black Hole Blues and Other Songs from Outer Space by Janna Levin; Knopf, 2016.

Warped Passages: Unraveling the Mysteries of the Universe's Hidden Dimensions by Lisa Randall; Ecco, 2006.

Black Holes and Time Warps: Einstein's Outrageous Legacy by Kip S. Thorne; Norton, 1994.

Quantum Computing Since Democritus by Scott Aaronson; Cambridge University Press, 2013.

A Quantum Computing Pamphlet by Dayton Ellwanger; Independently Published, 2019.

Possible Minds: Twenty-Five Ways of Looking at AI by John Brockman (Editor); Penguin Books, 2020.

The Singularity Is Near: When Humans Transcend Biology by Ray Kurzweil; Penguin Books, 2006.

Being You: A New Science of Consciousness by Anil Seth; Dutton, 2021.

Aliens: The World's Leading Scientists on the Search for Extraterrestrial Life by Jim Al-Khalili (Author, Editor); Picador, 2017.

Extraterrestrial: The First Sign of Intelligent Life Beyond Earth by Avi Loeb; Mariner Books, 2021.

The Mathematics of Love: Patterns, Proofs, and the Search for the Ultimate Equation (TED Books) by Hannah Fry; Simon & Schuster / TED, 2015.

Why We Love by Helen Fisher; Henry Holt & Co, 2004.

Bonk: The Curious Coupling of Science and Sex by Mary Roach; Norton, 2009.

Cycles of Time: An Extraordinary New View of the Universe by Roger Penrose; Vintage, 2012.

Brief Answers to the Big Questions by Stephen Hawking; Bantam, 2018.

The Jazz of Physics: The Secret Link Between Music and the Structure of the Universe by Stephon Alexander; Basic Books, 2016.

Entanglements: Tomorrow's Lovers, Families, and Friends (Twelve Tomorrows) by Sheila Williams (Editor); The MIT Press, 2020.

The End of Everything: (Astrophysically Speaking) by Katie Mack; Scribner, 2021.

ACKNOWLEDGMENTS

Thanks to my family, critique group, beta readers, editors, artists, designers, and everyone that helped make this book possible.

ABOUT THE AUTHOR

Gregory Allen Mendell has a PhD in physics, specializing in relativistic astrophysics. Besides splitting his time between various data and computing groups, he was fortunate to work with colleagues on many amazing gravitational-wave discoveries, including the first detection of these waves from a binary black hole merger. He has published a number of well-known research papers, taught, and worked in several countries. When writing science fiction, he explores human relationships and key mysteries about the future in stories filled with science and the search for love and hope. He enjoys spending time with his wife and family somewhere in the multiverse.

LINKS

https://www.amazon.com/author/gregoryallenmendell

STORIES

GREGORY ALLEN MENDELL

STORIES

GREGORY ALLEN MENDELL

STORIES

GREGORY ALLEN MENDELL

Made in United States
North Haven, CT
22 June 2023

38047107R00114